SKETCH

A YOUNG ADULT PSYCHOLOGICAL THRILLER

DIDI OVIATT

CHAPTER ONE

Michael wakes to the sound of drumming fingers on the wooden table next to his uncomfortable bunk. He rubs the sleep from his eyes and looks up to see his older brother John's face an inch from his, wide-eyed and impatient. John is one year older than Michael to the day. They both have shaggy black hair, a few freckles, and big green eyes. The only difference in appearance is that John is a few inches shorter, not nearly as muscular, and the gap between his front teeth is very noticeably larger. You'd never tell that Michael's the younger of the two. He's bigger, tougher, and meaner in every way. They're as close as twins, and look the part.

They share a cramped bedroom in a wooden shack of a home, in the middle of nowhere. Their sleepy farming town in central Montana isn't even big enough to make it on a map... any map. Being deep into a depression, there's no money to spare to fix the leaky roof, or busted windows. The walls are cracked, and floors are creaky.

"Michael, get your lazy butt out of bed."

Michael peaks out of the corner of his sleepy eyes, trying to process wakefulness. John has been sitting up next to him for a half an hour. He's been waiting for Michael to bounce to life, not daring to actually shake him awake, or yell. The last time John tried that, he got a fist to the face and had a black eye for a week. So instead, he's been sitting as close as he can get without actually touching his loudly snoring brother, just waiting.

"Jeez, it took you long enough. I've been waiting for hours." John lies.

Michael and John have been waiting on this day for over a month. Their best friend Steven spends the summer with his dad every year. Now that they're 16 and 17, practically all grown up, this will be the last summer they'll be able to spend with Steven for who knows how long. Times have been tough, and nothing seems to be lining up for improvement in the foreseeable future. The odds of Steven ever coming back to this place after the summer is slim.

Steven's father is one of the lucky men in the area who has been able to keep a job. He's a cashier at the one and only grocery/convenience store for miles. They sell everything from guns, to gas, to bread. It's a small store, but it has every essential any passer-through may need for survival.

Not many people in town have the money for food. For the most part, they poach small game, and find their own way of living. But the area does seem to get a lot of drifters. There's a small room that's rented out in the back of the store. Steven's father has been the keeper of the place since the boys can remember.

Michael slowly sits up, stretching his arms as far as they can go in the lack of space their bedroom allows.

"Hold your horses, John. God, you can be such a butt-hole sometimes."

Michael doesn't handle being woken up very well. He isn't a morning person, and his short temper is at an all-time high within the first hour that he rolls to his feet. There's been a mean streak in Michael's blood since he was knee high to his mommy, pulling on her apron for attention. He's been known as the fighter of his class every year since the first year he went to school. Resorting to fists has been his favorite thing to do since he can remember. Over the years, he's progressed into quite the scrappy teen.

Michael has learned to save his fighting for after school, so that there are no teachers around to get him in trouble. The Hounds boys work odd jobs on local farms and gardening at home, but they spend most of their time hunting. They sell or trade the firs from their kills for anything that can be used to take care of themselves and their sick mom.

Not having a father at home made them learn to take care of themselves and at young age. It's also made their mom very good at finding strange but effective punishments when either of them got into trouble growing up.

"Well, you boys are too big for a small woman like me to be whoopin' ya, so I guess I'll have to find some other way to teach you a lesson."

She'd say this before taking them door to door, asking everyone they came in contact with if the boys could scrub their floors and wash their windows. It's always been disgusting and humiliating enough to teach the boys a lesson. Mrs. Hounds is by no means a weak woman. She's been raising Michael and John by herself since they were babies. Their father took off without a word. No explanation or excuses, he just up and left.

"That man was no good anyway, we're all better off without him."

It's all their mother had said on the matter. Now that she's sick, they have little to no time for fights or playing around.

In no time at all, Michael and John have their shoes and hats on. Their lunches are packed, and they're out the door. It's a long walk to Steven's house. They only have one peddle bike between the two of them, so they opt to leave it behind. Some people call it the boonies, some call it redneck hills, and some the Sticks. To the Hounds and the other twenty or so families that live in this spaced-out little farming community, it's home. It's an adventurous place with lots to explore and get into.

Mrs. Hounds was gone most of the time while the boys were

growing up. She worked long hours as a nurse at the little clinic at the edge of town. She decided they were old enough at 11 and 12 to get through the summers without a babysitter, given they would check in at the neighbors at least once a day. It was a hard decision for her, but she really couldn't afford to pay for childcare. Especially with the price of heat and food, they struggled enough as it was.

So, at only 11 and 12, Michael and John had the freedom that most kids their age only dreamed of. They caused a lot of trouble and learned to take care of themselves. It paid off in the long run, as now they're not only taking care of themselves, but their mother too.

"We have to stop and see if Chloe changed her mind," says Michael.

Chloe lives a half a mile in the opposite direction from Steven's house. Obviously, John isn't happy about the idea.

"Hell no! We're not going to get your stupid girlfriend. She doesn't even like Steven and she already said 'there was no way in hell she was walking half a day to meet up with some dumb kid with a big mouth,' remember?"

John actually likes Chloe, and he knows how mad Michael gets when he labels her with the girlfriend title. Right now, he doesn't care.

"Well, you do whatever you want, but I'm going to get her."

Michael doesn't do much without Chloe. He takes off toward her house, knowing that John won't argue with him much further. Being the younger of the two doesn't stop Michael from getting his point across by any means. John rolls his eyes and follows with his head dropped to his chest. There's no point in fighting about it. Kicking rocks along the way, John keeps a close distance in the rear.

It only takes about ten minutes before they're knocking on the giant wooden door to the front entrance of Chloe's house. It swings open with a woosh, and there she stands. Her long, bleached from the sun, blonde hair is pulled into a ponytail that falls into the middle of her back. She's wearing a light pink tank top with matching shoes. Chloe is short and slim with an hourglass shape. At first glance one could easily think her to be the proper, private school type... until she talks.

"What in Sam's hell are you two dirtbags doin' at my house so early in the mornin'? I thought you were goin' to hang out with that pig you call a friend." She grips a hand on her hip. "If you think your gunna' guilt me into walkin' all the way to his cow shit smellin' crap-hole just because you came out of your way to get me. You must be slow in the head."

Chloe doesn't have much of a filter in what she says, never has. And, she sure doesn't have the time or desire to be proper. She rolls her eyes at the two filthy Hounds boys standing on her giant porch filled with flowers and wicker decor. She quickly decides that she'd rather go on an adventure and play in the mud at some point, than sit at home with her parents' maid. Her parents travel on business most of the summers and leave her alone with a jolly, oversized woman who speaks little English. Living in a depression makes no difference to the Mead family. They have 'old money' and aren't afraid to show it.

Despite their efforts to make Chloe a snob much like them, she put her foot down at a very early age. Chloe refused private school and has a mind of her own. Eventually they gave up and let her do her own thing, turning a blind eye to her in the process.

"I'll be back by dark!" Chloe yells into the house.

She slams the door, stomps past them onto the road, and takes the lead to their 'stupid friend's house'.

Chloe's house is the only one of its size within a five-county range, and it's the only one of its size that the Hounds boys have ever seen. None of the others who live in the area really understand why the Meads built such a place there. They're never home and they don't fit in. Really, no one with more than a couple dollars saved up in pennies does.

Chloe doesn't care. She fits in just fine, and she loves it there. Which is probably the reason Michael likes to be around her so much. So does John, even though he'd never admit it out loud.

Michael decided the day that Chloe put a water snake in their teacher's drawer, ultimately resulting in her screaming, running out of the room and practically peeing her pants, that Chloe was probably the funniest girl he'd ever meet. Not only that, but she's all spit and grit. Chloe isn't one bit afraid of Michael's temper. She's reminded him of that on a daily basis, practically their whole lives.

One time he got mad at her for drilling him in the ear with a dirt clod. They were supposed to be on the same team in an all-out playground war. When he got to yelling at her, she told him, "Michael Hounds, I'll give you a pass on this one, but if you ever yell at me like this again, don't you think I won't be afraid to kick you as hard as I can between the legs and then run circles around you. You'll feel it for a week and you'll never catch me!"

He knew she wasn't joking because he'd seen her do it before. Every kid in school knew that she was the fastest around on foot.

The three of them take off toward Steven's house, having what they think will be great timing. Then, after about a ten-minute walk, Chloe unexpectedly takes a risky turn. The wooded area she disappears into is thick and darkened by the shadowing trees.

"Hey maybe we should stick to the road this time," shouts John.

"Yeah Chloe, remember what happened last time we took a shortcut?" Michael mocks, "John got a tiny scratch on his leg and cried like a baby."

He ducks into the darkness, leaving John to stand alone on the road for a few seconds before running after them. John is afraid to get too far behind them, just in case he gets lost. He loves the woods just as much as the other two, but only on one condition. John is extremely cautious, and always makes sure that he can at least see, or hear, who ever he's with.

"It wasn't a tiny scratch, you dick. Mom had to put six stitches in my thigh, remember?"

John keeps on ranting and raving while he follows his younger and much braver brother, along with his all too crazy girlfriend into the woods. John is a great aim with his rifle, and awesome at skinning deer, but when it comes to exploring new places, he's definitely not the type to lead the way. After years of running into bear and being stalked by mountain lions, he's developed a slight fear of getting caught up alone in the wilderness. That's not to mention the deep-rooted terror of wolves that's instilled into his blood, despite the fact that he's yet to actually see one.

The woods get thicker and thicker. They have to climb over the dead fallen trees, tread through small muddy ponds, and avoid the giant holes in the ground. All the while, not knowing what kind of wild animals might be lurking nearby.

"Snake!" yells Chloe.

The thick trees open up into a small grassy flat, and Chloe sprints into it like a cheetah. One thing about Chloe is that she loves to catch snakes.

"Don't be stupid Chloe, that sucker's huge!" shouts Michael, as he reluctantly chases after her.

Michael hates snakes, he never really can tell them apart. Not knowing if they're poisonous or not scares the crap out of him. Every time they come across one, he's convinced it's going to sink its fangs in and put one of them into the ground forever. Chloe laughs at him before pulling out the pocket knife she keeps tied to her belt for just such an occasion. Then she dives into the tall grass.

By the time John and Michael catch up to her in the middle of the flat, she has cut the head off the biggest snake they've seen her kill yet. She's starting to gather a small stack of sticks and bark, placing them on a mound of sandy mud.

"Well, ain't you dirtbags gunna' help me build a fire? I didn't pack no fancy sandwich in any stupid little pack like you two sissy lala's. I'm havin' this juicy snake for lunch. Ain't ya' gettin' hungry?"

It drives John crazy that Chloe's favorite way to refer to him is a dirtbag. Nonetheless, they head back out of the flat to pick up all of the dead wood they can carry back. Soon enough, a fire is blazing and the only smell around is that of the long-skinned serpent wrapped around Chloe's makeshift roasting stick. She holds it over the fire and watches the meat sizzle and drip. Surprisingly, it smells like chicken and both the Hounds brothers can't help themselves but to have a taste.

It doesn't take long after their brunch is devoured that the three hoodlums are stepping out of the deep woods and back onto a road. As the sun continues to rise in the sky, it leaves on the pavement a sweltering heat. It's only a short walk longer to Steven's house, and the luxury of water will be welcomed.

"See, told ya it wouldn't be so bad," says Michael, as he turns to his brother and flashes a smug grin. "We didn't even see any other animals, and we ate some pretty awesome tastin' snake."

John can't argue with that. Though he isn't entirely convinced that the shortcut took any time off their trip, considering they had to move much slower, climbing over and ducking through all the irritating deadfall. Usually Steven meets them halfway down the long windy road on his bike. The last couple years they've had to spend more time working than hanging out with Steven, it's made things very different.

That's why today they decided to take the time away from of their chores and surprise Steven when he got into town. Chloe and Steven have always butted heads more than they get along. John swears it's because Steven secretly has the hots for her. But he'd never say it out loud for fear of setting off Michael.

"Steven!" both boys shout as they run through his yard, and meet him at the porch.

Chloe stands her ground on the driveway with her arms crossed. Her eyes roll a full circle.

"I see you brought your snappy sidekick." Steven says, glancing over at her.

She sticks out her tongue and sneers.

"Glad you're still as ugly as you were last summer, Steven."

CHAPTER TWO

It's a hot and sweaty day. Steven's been back for a couple of weeks now. Just like every other summer, the four spend little time outside of their jobs away from one another. They're kicked back on Steven's porch eating ice cream. The Hounds brothers have been out of bed since before the sun came up, digging ditches and fixing fences.

The small cushioned seat of the rickety porch swing and the cold ice cream in their mouths is a welcomed treat. Ice cream is rare. Steven's father found an old barrel hidden in the back of the freezer in the store. It had too much frost on the top to sell to any passersby, so he was allowed to take it home and share with his family. Now, here they sit, enjoying the day. They're waiting for Mr. Smith to leave for work so they can get into the basement.

Chloe figured out how to pick a lock with the pins from her hair years ago, so that she could get into her father's office while he was gone, which sadly, is still more often than not. Her father's oversized office is his favorite hiding place for any trinkets having been taken away from Chloe. By the time she gets into the room and steals them back, he never remembers what he had hidden anyway in the first place.

The first time Chloe broke into his office, it was to steal a few boxes of shotgun shells and .22 bullets for Michael. Her father had purchased them in bulk to save a few bucks. She was twelve at the time. While Chloe was in the room, she also found all the pocket knives, critter traps, and blow dart guns that had also been taken away from her... this sparked an inferno of breaking and entering.

Chloe decided that very day, that she wanted to pick every lock they come across, just to see what was behind it. The boys all loved her new talent. They were able to acquire lots of forbidden treasures, and no one ever knew what they were missing. They'd all been taught from birth not to steal. But to the Hounds brothers and their two closest friends, rules are just not something they're interested in.

They have a shed built deep into the woods that no one would possibly be crazy enough to enter. This is where they've stashed their treasure for years. They have guns, fleshing knives, saws, spray paint, rope of all lengths, and even small pieces of furniture. Practically anything that could be carried and that they knew would not be missed. Most of all from Chloe's place. They all just figure that's the beauty of living in a gigantic house full of crap that you don't need, and most likely would ever notice has gone missing.

As soon as Steven's dad, Robert Smith, pulls down the road, they look mischievously at one another and then take off in a sprint down the steps into his basement. Steven has always wanted to know what's locked away down here. His father told him years ago that it was just a room full of old newspapers. But Steven's always known there has to be more to this dingy-looking door all locked away. It doesn't take Chloe long to pick the lock. She's getting better and faster at it with every lock she opens. The door creaks, and there it is.

"Holy shit," gasps John.

"This is the best day of my life," says Michael.

"Look at the dust on all this stuff. I'll bet this door hasn't been open in years! No one will even notice if we take it!" adds Chloe.

Steven whispers in fear, "I don't know guys, my dad will kill me if he finds out."

"No, he won't, Red, I can take him," jokes Michael.

Staring back at them from the wall to wall metal storage shelves are two small crossbows and an open chest of arrows. Along with old war paint, hatchets, a couple machetes and rope. There is one box of newspapers setting on the floor.

"What the hell was my dad doing with this stuff?" Steven asks, more to himself than the others.

Steven's dad isn't an adventurous man, and aside from the yearly deer and occasional bear he shoots, he doesn't even like to get out and do much.

"The bears are getting out of control around here," and, "we gotta' have meat to survive," is his logic for hunting.

He doesn't enjoy hunting as a sport like the majority of other men and even women in town. It's more of a chore for him, which is only one step away from insanity from Steven's point of view. Hunting is Steven's favorite thing to do with his dad, aside from throwing a football.

"Who cares *why* he has this stuff!?" John says, always the planner of the group. "Let's just take it now and hurry, in case he forgot something and has to come back home. We don't want to get caught carrying it all out of your house."

They grab as much as they can lift and head straight for the woods. Distracted by all the cool things, they don't even bother to glance at the newspapers in the box on the floor.

"This is awesome! I get to shoot one first," shouts Chloe, grabbing the black one.

"And I get the other one first," follows Michael, staking his claim on the green one.

"Oh hell no! They're my dads, I get to shoot one first."

Steven can't help but to fight for this one. He hasn't been this excited and scared, all at the same time in all of his sixteen years.

Michael has nothing else to say, and he refuses let Steven take ahold of his new weapon. Michael holds the crossbow to his side and throws a powerful swing at Steven with his free hand. Being friends with Michael means you're bound to get into a fight or two, so you have to be able to take a punch.

Steven is no pansy and he isn't a little guy by any means. His shaggy red hair goes flying to the side as his jaw takes the blow of the hit. Steven doesn't much care if this is a fight he can win or lose, he jumps in with fists swinging. Quicker than the crossbow can hit the ground, John swoops in to grab it. He and Chloe stand to the side, waiting for one of them to knock the other out or wrestle one another into submission.

"My money's on Steven this time. I think he's had a growth spurt since the last time they got into it. Even his fists are bigger." Chimes in Chloe, watching intently with her own fists balled.

"You're on, Blondie. My brother never has lost a fight to Steven," replies John matter of factly. "If he loses, you have to skin the next ten rabbits I shoot."

"And, if Steven wins?"

"I won't tell Michael that I catch you staring at him all the time."

Chloe's heart skips a beat, and she lowers her eyes at him.

"Deal," she agrees, reaching her hand out to give John's a firm shake.

The fight doesn't last long. A little bobbing and weaving, and the next thing they know Steven is knocked out on the ground. Chloe splashes a little water on his face and helps him up with a struggled pull.

"You're lucky he didn't break your nose this time," she tells him.

Chloe giggles, helps guide Steven back up to his wobbling feet, and then over to a nearby boulder. She steadies his shoulders while he sits down with a huff. Chloe enjoys seeing Steven get a beating once in a while, she thinks he has it coming. She especially enjoys seeing Michael do the beating. She could watch him fight every day of the week, it never gets old. Chloe has secretly had a thing for

Michael since they were little, but she always figured he never saw her that way. She accepted how close they are as friends, and has never told or shown him that she's felt any different. She doesn't want anyone to think she's some sort of sissy lala for having those type feelings anyway.

After the few minutes it takes Steven to regain his strength and thought process, Michael hands him the weapon.

"You sure do have some giant red kahunas, Steven Smith," he teases as he gives the crossbow up.

Anyone willing to take a punch like that over a dumb ol' bow probably deserves to shoot it first anyway, Michael thinks. Plus, he knows that if he really wanted to shoot one first all he'd have to do is wink at Chloe and she'd hand hers over in a heartbeat.

For being the loudest and toughest girl he knows, she sure isn't very good at hiding the way she blushes when he gives her certain looks or says certain things. Michael loves that she has no clue how much he notices her. To him, she's like having a steaming mug of hot cocoa hidden away for no one else but himself to enjoy on rainy days. Once her teeth were no longer too big for her smile and the rest of her body grew into the size of her feet and hands, she became quite an attractive young woman. Any guy their age would be a fool not to notice.

Michael has always known she'd be his one day, but he does want to 'get to know' other girls before he's ready to settle down with Chloe. So he's decided not to let her in on his not so little plans for their big future together, just yet. In the meantime, he assumes that they'll stay the same as they always have, until he's ready for the rest of his life.

Their day, full of shooting the new-found toys, turns into weeks of much anticipated target practice before and after working on the farms. Soon, they have plenty of experience under their belts, and are each getting to be an awesome shot. It has become a part of their regular routine. It has only taken about three weeks and any squirrel, pigeon, rabbit, or badger within sight stands no chance. The larger game like deer and elk are a bit tougher to get close enough to for a good shot, but each of them is determined. It has grown to be a standing bet on who will nail the first one.

It's a day like any other, Michael and Chloe are crouched down behind a fallen tree. They have mud caked on their flesh an inch thick. Mud is hands down the best camouflage. Not only does it hide them from sight, but from smell too. Fresh coyote tracks have been in this spot almost every day for the last week. The two sit in perfect silence, just waiting, as they have several times before, stalking an animal. That's when they see it.

The biggest bear either of them have ever come across slowly makes its way to a pond, just a few yards away from them. The hair on the animal is thick and dark brown. Its paws leave tracks the size of dinner plates. They set their sights.

It's Chloe who pulls the trigger first, and Michael nearly in unison.

"Got him!" She yells.

Chloe jumps up as soon as the arrows strike fur. But rather than the bear dropping like the small game they've killed in the past, or running off to die within minutes like it would have if it were shot with a gun, the bear stands its ground. It is pissed... roaring ferociously and swiping its huge paws around in the dirt.

"No!" Michael yells as the bear storms toward them. "Shit, run Chloe run!"

They take off in the opposite direction. The bear's gaining ground, and quick.

"Hurry, in the tree!" Chloe shouts as she starts up the base of a huge oak tree. Michael is right behind her.

"What are we doing Chloe? Bears can climb trees too, you idiot!" He yells at her while he's scaling the branches like an ape.

As fast as humanly possible they scurry up the tree, branch for branch. Luckily, the bear is hit and wounded. It's unable to lift itself up the trunk. Putting its front paws at the base of the tree, it bawls and bawls. It's three-inch-long claws ravish the bark violently. It's close enough to the two that they can smell the horrendous breath and see the steam pouring from out of its mouth.

"Oh my God, look at the size of its teeth," Michael points out.

"I wonder how long it's gunna' take him to die?"

"I don't know, we could be up here all night," he says, peeking at her slyly out of the corner of his eye.

"Crap." Chloe blushes, trying not to look back at him.

By the time the sun goes down, the bear is laying in a heap a few yards away. The smell of it is so strong, that both Michael and Chloe have been breathing into their muddy clothes for hours. They've eaten all the jerky out of their pockets and have drunk every last drop of water from their canteens.

They sit at the top of the tree, watching the beast pace back and forth while it waits for them to come down. It stares up at them occasionally, eyes glowing with anger. It chatters and clicks its teeth in warning every time they move around, and swats the ground with its enormous paws. Eventually its footsteps slow down and its breath grows shallow. Until finally, it collapses. They wait a while, just in case he isn't completely dead before they climb down from the tree.

"We better get outta' here before it gets any darker. Who knows what the smell of its dead body is gunna' attract in the dark." Michael says.

"We can't just leave it here, maybe we should at least skin it." She says.

"Are you crazy, or just stupid? We're an hour from home and it's already gettin' dark."

"Fine then. But if anything happens to it between now and the mornin' I'm gunna' shoot *you* with this stupid bow too." Chloe threatens.

As a part of their compromise, Michael convinces Chloe to sleep the night on his couch so they can all go back to the pond early and get what they can of the bear in the daylight. They'd need to quarter the meat, hitch a ride to the county over and trade it all at the market for medical supplies, milk, wheat and rice. Its bound to be a full day's project, so they'd need to get to it as early as possible. They should be able to get more than a month's worth of supplies from the bear's hide alone. That's not to mention the meat, and claws.

Chloe offers to steal money from her father to support the Hounds family on a regular basis, but they refuse take the dishonest handout. So instead, she's usually forced to shut up and help them earn a keep. They'd need to get the bear completely taken care of and sold at market before late afternoon when they'd be needed to feed and water the cows and chickens at a few surrounding farms.

After stashing the bows in their nearby secret spot, they haul butt in the dark to the Hounds' home. With a vicious blend of excitement and exhaustion from the day, Michael falls asleep as soon as they're back and his head hits his pillow. Chloe is in and out all night. She can't seem to rest easily, with her mind drifting from thoughts of the bear to those of Michael, sitting next to her on a branch of the tree.

She can't stop thinking of the way their arms and legs touched, having to squish together so closely. She replays his comment of staying there all night over and over in her head. She imagines how it would be if he would just kiss her randomly during one of their adventures, and she wonders if he ever would. For a while, Chloe contemplates climbing in bed with him just to feel him breathe. She wonders what it would be like to hold his hand on their hikes, and to feel his arm around the small of her back while they sit outside in the dark, finding constellations in the stars.

Although she's well aware of how sappy she is, thinking all of these girly romantic thoughts, Chloe just can't help herself. She thinks about what their kids might look like, and even recites the name over and over in her head 'Chloe Hounds, Chloe Hounds, Chloe Hounds. She loves the way it sounds.

After a while lying there, unable to sleep, Chloe starts to get angry at herself, knowing she's going to have to wake up in just a couple hours. All that she really wants to do is go home, take a bath, and sleep in her nice clean bed. Though, even at home she'd probably wear one of Michael's tee-shirts to sleep in, she usually does. Chloe has a collection of Michael's clothes that's been stolen from him over the years. *He'll never know it was me,* she convinces herself every time.

CHAPTER THREE

Bang! Bang! Bang! Upon jumping a few feet off the couch, Chloe wakes to the sound of someone pounding on the door. She races to answer it, not thinking of what she has on. The door swings open with a creek to reveal Mr. Crawl from down the lane. Mr. Crawl is a tall skinny man with a slight hunch in his back and a limp. He's in his mid-forties but looks more like late-fifties. His skin is full of wrinkles and his hair is peppered with grey.

"Where the hell is she?" He shouts.

"Who?" Chloe demands.

"My daughter! She never came home last night and I know these crazy sons of bitchin Hounds boys are just the type to take her! Just like that killer takin' girls years back." He yells, "I know that John kid's been eyein' her down lately and I'm gunna' kill him!"

"Now wait just a doggon' minute, you stupid old man."

Now Chloe is upset.

Upsetting Chloe isn't something you want to do, considering Michael is like her own personal guard dog. With the tone of Chloe's voice waking Michael, he bolts out of bed and to the door. He stops in his tracks at the sight of her, standing there in his old tee-shirt and boxers. She wasn't about to sleep in her nasty dried up muddy pants and a shirt, stinking like sweat and dead animal. She'd snuck into his room while he slept and swiped something clean and comfortable to snooze in.

Ignoring the screaming old man at the door, all Michael can do is stare at this beautiful angry crush, who's standing in his living room, dressed in practically nothing but his shirt. Her hair is a mess, tangled and wild. Unable to take his eyes off Chloe, and the smirk off his mouth, Michael only hears about half of their bickering back and forth. Before long, Chloe screams at the man, calling him every name in the book. She refuses to let him through the door. It isn't until Mr. Crawl calls her a 'stupid shit liar' that Michael pulls himself out of the trance and is able to assess the situation.

"Now, calm down, Sir. Let's talk about this rationally, and outside on a lower level. My mom is sick and trying to rest."

It's a surprising response from Michael, but one thing the Hounds boys have learned from their mother is respect for their elders. Michael has done a lot of work over the years for Mr. Crawl and knows how to deal with him on a personal level. Mr. Crawl also has a great deal of respect for Mrs. Hounds. Despite his anger and accusations, the least he can do is let the sick woman sleep.

"That brother of yours took my baby girl Misty, and I'm gunna' get him." Mr. Crawl argues.

His voice is an octave lower than before, but the hatred in his fiery eyes burns strong.

Misty is a couple of years older than John. She has short dark hair and is a bit on the plump side. Though most girls are married off, and some even with a child by the time they're Misty's age, she's refused. John has been madly in love with her for years but never had the nerve to approach her.

"I've seen the way he stares at her, I ain't stupid! She never came home last night. Now let me in your house so I can have a look for myself."

Mr. Crawl starts stomping toward the house.

By putting one hand out to the old man's chest, Michael stops him in his tracks. Young or not, he nearly doubles the old man in size.

"I'm sorry sir, I can't let you go stomping around my house waking up my mom and accusing my sleeping brother of something so outrageous."

Michael is just as firm as he needs to be, and stands his ground.

"I know my brother didn't do anything wrong, because he was asleep in his bed when I got home last night, and he is still asleep in the same place now."

"He did it before you got here then! Who the hell else would it've been?"

"Mr. Crawl..." Michael tries to interject, but is cut off.

"I know you boys are as crazy as sin. I know there'd be no stopping you, if you set your mind to an innocent little girl like my Misty."

Spit flies, and Mr. Crawl's face pinches tighter and tighter with every word.

"Now, you listen here old man," yells Chloe. "Ain't no way John would want that smelly ol' cow girl of yours! She is ugly as a man's ass!"

Michael rolls his eyes, and releases an exasperated sigh. Mr. Crawl is fuming.

"Chloe, why don't you go make sure John's not wakin' up." Michael tells her. "If he is, tell him to stay in the house for a while 'till I come in. I'm gunna' have a talk with Mr. Crawl here."

John is wide awake now, standing just inside the doorway with his hair in a sleepy woosh to one side. He's holding his shotgun, cocked and loaded, ready to fire if needs be. He isn't about to let some nut job come storming into his house accusing him of anything. John loves Misty, and would never do anything to hurt her. If Mr. Crawl only knew how he felt, maybe he wouldn't be making such crazy accusations.

"John, what the hell you gunna' do with that?" Chloe demands.

"I didn't do nothin', Chloe." John's voice is steady, and quiet as the wind. "If he comes in here yellin' at me, I'm gunna' shoot him in the leg."

"John, don't go doin' nothin' stupid. We all know you didn't take that fat pig," Chloe says.

"Don't call her that, Chloe." John says a little louder, careful not to be heard by Misty's dad outside the door.

"Wow, you really do like her, don't ya'?"

Chloe's brows pull together in the middle, and she tilts her head to the side.

"What do you care? Maybe you should shut your big mouth, Chloe. If someone took her, I'm gunna' find 'em and kill 'em myself," he says.

Chloe takes a breath, looks deeply into his intense eyes, and can tell without a doubt that he's serious. She doesn't want to push him any further. John's like a brother to her and she knows if he actually cares for this girl, then she'd better accept it and help him out if she can. Chloe stands up a little straighter and puts an arm around John.

"We'll find her," she tells him.

John stands strong, holding tightly to the wooden stock of his weapon. All the while Michael is doing his best to calm down and talk some sense into the loud, out of his mind Mr. Crawl outside. Chloe hurries off to find some clean clothes of Mrs. Hounds' to wear, determined not to miss anything.

John sets down the gun and collapses onto the couch, holding his head in his hands. Images of Misty's emerald eyes staring at him as they passed by one another, or of her smile when he caught her laughing with her friends, is all he can focus on. *What if she really is gone? What if some crazy drifter took off with her? What if she is dead?*

John can't force all the frightening thoughts out of his head. *I should have just told her how I felt. I should have told her how beautiful the sound of her voice is. I should have let her know how I get a chill every time I hear her laughing.* John has so many things running through his mind, he can't keep it straight. Worry, anger and wonder grab a tight hold on him from deep in his belly to the tips of his toes.

Chloe walks back into the room all dressed and clean. All she can do is stare at him on the couch. She's always known John is the softer of the two Hounds brothers, but she's still never seen him look so vulnerable. It's like looking at a lost child. *How could they not have noticed he had a thing for the girl down the road?* She makes a vow to herself that she won't give up until Misty's found. She'd sell everything in her parent's house and travel as far as she had to, to find the damn girl if that's what it takes.

Chloe hates to see John looking so lost and hurt. What could've possibly happened for Misty to take off without saying a word? She isn't the type of girl to run around with random guys or even talk to passers-by. Misty is always close to her friends and her father. She seems to be a fairly happy girl, even in all the hard times. Chloe has to help find her, for John.

Michael manages to convince Mr. Crawl to join him in a walk to the neighbors down the way. His hopes are high that their car is in working order and actually has gas. There aren't many vehicles around. The few people in town who do own one can hardly afford gas or parts to fix anything broken. The Victor's place is less than a mile away, it's their best bet. Michael is urging Mr. Crawl to go right to the Sheriff, rather than taking matters into his own hands. Michael knows a little walk, and a little time, might calm Mr. Crawl down some. They are lucky, and are able to hitch a ride from Mrs. Victor into town.

The old pickup slows to a stop in front of a one-story aging brick building, with a wooden sign over the door that reads, 'The Station'. Michael thanks Mrs. Victor kindly while they step out of the single, bucket seat cab. Mr. Crawl marches straight to the Deputy. He's kicked back on wooden rocking chair, guarding the building's only door.

"Where's the Sheriff?" Mr. Crawl demands. "He inside there? I gotta' bone ta' pick."

"He jumped on Ol' blue 'bout ten minutes back, not sure which way he went," Deputy Evan mumbles back, before spitting a long string of brown slime from his chaw.

Deputy Evan is a very tall man with chicken legs and a round belly. He's not in shape and doesn't care much about his smell. Even the dirtiest men in town can't stand to be around him. The scent is enough to make any average man lose their appetite. Sheriff Black spends more time on his giant brown and white paint horse than he does anywhere else. No one knows why he calls the horse Ol' blue, there's nothing blue about him.

Deputy Evan nods and listens as Mr. Crawl gives him a quick rundown of Misty's lost whereabouts. Without a word, he slowly pulls himself to his full six-foot four height and disappears into the building. The town alarm sounds. A giant bell on top of the jailhouse is the only way of group communication in the town. Its reserved for only the biggest of emergencies.

The last time Michael could remember the sound of the bell is when he was 5 years old and someone had lit the clinic on fire. Blew it up was more like it. Luckily, his mom wasn't hurt in the incident, but there were two victims that died in the explosion. It was the largest fire most people in town had ever seen, and they never did catch the culprit. Someone had thrown a stick of dynamite into a window.

Mrs. Hounds had walked out to get some air after seeing the shape of a patient that had entered the building. As she was opening the front door to go back inside, the explosion happened in the back half of the clinic. The dynamite had been thrown into the window where the poor girl was being treated. The young woman had been attacked and was covered in blood.

Apparently, she was yet be identified and she had stab wounds all over her body. There was one doctor in the room with her at the time of the explosion. The receptionist was out to lunch. Mrs. Hounds was the only other person around, and she had to gather herself before going back into the clinic to assist with treatment. Just as she opened the door, the *boom* took place. It blew her a few feet back and the building burned to the ground. Mrs. Hounds hadn't told the boys many details about the incident.

"That's not a matter for children, I've told you all you need to know," is all she would report every time the subject came up.

As the bell rings now, a chill rushes through Michael's veins. It's beginning to sink in how serious the matter is, and it's leaving an empty hole in the pit of his stomach. He's spent the last half an hour trying to calm down an old man who's daughter has gone missing. But, until this moment, he hasn't actually had a chance to absorb the situation. Thus far, Michael has assumed that it has got to be something simple. Like perhaps she's merely wandered into the woods and gotten lost. This happens now and again to various people around here. No matter how familiar one is with the woods, it isn't hard to get turned around. Something is whispering in his ear that with Misty, being lost isn't the case.

The townsmen start to gather before the jailhouse door. Concern and panic are plastered on all of their faces as they walk, run, and ride their horses in. The Sheriff must not have been far. He's the first to arrive. Trying to get just far enough away to avoid the smell of Evan, most likely. He listens closely to an increasingly panicked and angry Mr. Crawl, and asks him every detail he can remember.

The Sheriff wraps the rains of his horse around a tall pole next to the jailhouse. He adjusts his belt and looks around at the growing crowd. The first question in mind is, why had Deputy Evan rung the bell before they could determine if Misty hadn't gotten lost? It seemed a bit unnecessary to create a panic. If he'd have been there rather than Deputy Evan, he would have handled things a little differently. Sheriff Black would have just taken a few townsfolk out, looking for the girl before he alerted and panicked the town. But the deed was done, and now the crowd is growing.

Mr. Crawl explains to the Sheriff, along with the growing audience, that Misty is extremely afraid of the woods and that she'd never wander off the road, especially by herself. He tells how rare it is for her to walk alone, even just to the store. It is very out of character for Misty to be all by herself. Mr. Crawl explains to the Sheriff that he'd yelled at her the day before. He'd told her that she needed to grow up and start doing things and going places on her own. Mr. Crawl had gotten mad at Misty for always having to be accompanied by him or a friend and sent her to the store on purpose... by herself.

Mr. Crawl is confident that Misty would've stuck to the road and never wandered off into the trees all alone. Mr. Crawl had assumed that Misty stayed at a friend's house because she was upset with him. It wasn't until this morning, when there was still no word from her, that he started to panic. He'd checked a few of her friends' houses, and when none of them had heard from her either, he knew something had to have happened.

It quickly becomes clear to Sheriff Black why the old farmer is in such a panic. It has been a long time since there was anything out of the ordinary here. There had been several girls gone missing and murdered years before. The killer was never found. Though it all happened so long ago, the Sheriff remembers it like it was yesterday. He'd helped on the search when one of the women was recovered. They'd found her strung up from a tree with more than a dozen arrows stuck into her body and the trunk of the tree she was hanging from. Even after all this time the Sheriff can still remember every detail.

As the crowd continues to grow bigger, Sheriff Black starts to organize a search plan. He draws out a map of the surrounding wooded areas in the dirt with a stick, before separating the crowd into a few search groups. The townsfolk part, each group with a direction and a plan. They're all to keep their eyes peeled and look for any sort of clue as to what might have happened to Misty. All they can do is search for something, anything, and pray to find her alive.

There are two passers-by who have been staying in the small room at the store for the last couple of days. They are taken into custody to be held and questioned as soon as possible. The Sheriff doesn't want to take any chances of them leaving town, if they have any information. The women are ordered to keep their children indoors and a weapon on hand.

Chloe and John jog into the crowd, out of breath and gasping as the people are finishing up their game plans.

"There's the miserable son of a bitch who took her!" yells Mr. Crawl.

All heads turn to stare at John as he jogs to the Sheriff to proclaim his innocence.

"Now, now, let's not jump to pointing fingers just yet." Sheriff Black steps between Mr. Crawl and John. "She could have gotten lost in the woods for all we know."

A farmer's wife stands a couple feet away from Mr. Crawl. She speaks up loudly and confidently on John's behalf.

"You know if this has anything to do with all those girls years ago, there is no way that young Hounds boy could have taken her! You remember Ruth Ann just as well as I do, Crawl. She grew up down the road from you and she was taken from her bed in the middle of the night. These Hounds boys would've been babies then."

She stares down the old farmer from under lowered brows. He instantly hangs his head.

"Either way, son, I'll need you to stick around so we can ask you a few questions on the matter before you join the search party." Sheriff Black says quietly to John.

John nods in agreement. He wants to ask his own questions, and is eager to be in the same room while they interrogate the outsiders. John isn't in his right mind, and isn't thinking of what kind of disaster the Sheriff and Deputy Evan's interrogations can be.

"If you're gunna' be pokin' around botherin' my brother, then I'm stayin' too," jumps in Michael.

He's not about to leave while they drill and most likely beat his brother into submission. He knows how dirty and dishonest the law around here can be, especially Sheriff Black and Deputy Evan. Michael has landed himself into this jailhouse on a couple of occasions after getting into fights or stealing alcohol.

He knows how Sheriff Black and Deputy Evan are capable of acting so nicely and understandingly, when they're around the public, and then turn around and slam you in the back of your head with the butt of a pistol when no one's looking. Once unconscious you aren't aware of the kicking to the ribs or the bar to your legs until you come-to and can feel nothing but sheer pain to various parts of your body.

Michael knows, better than anyone, the Sheriff's ways of making people talk. Even his ways of making people admit to doing things they didn't actually do, just to close a case. The Sheriff and Deputy of this town are a nasty couple, and no one in their right minds would leave a family member behind to be questioned alone. Sheriff Black stares back at Michael with a cold and nasty glare. His lips slowly turn up into a callous grin.

"Be my guest, we could use all the Hounds' information we can get."

Steven and his father, Robert, are standing to the back of the crowd listening intently to any piece of information they might be able to use. Chloe joins them in their stance while Michael and John enter the jailhouse. The rest of the townsfolk part ways in all directions, guns in hand, and ready themselves for any outcome.

The women also disperse, making their way home with their children. Most of the men are in an outrage, determined to find Misty. Comments are coming from every direction as they separate and scatter like organized schools of fish.

"We're gunna kill the son of a bitch", "He better pray she is still alive", "Whatever is done to Misty we we'll do to whoever got her," and, "this kinda' thing doesn't happen around here, we won't stand for it."

The comments and rage are shared by nearly every abled body. Everyone except for Steven and Chloe. All they can do is gawk at the jailhouse as Sheriff Black and Deputy Evan follow the Hounds boys in and close the door.

CHAPTER FOUR

"I'm not leavin' 'til they come out," states Steven, standing his ground.

"Me either! If we hear screamin' were breakin' the doors down," agrees Chloe.

"I don't think that's a very good idea, kids." Robert says. "Those boys can handle themselves. We don't want to make the situation any worse than it already is."

Steven's father keeps a level head, though he doesn't move from his stance either. Curiosity seems to have frozen him in place. Dumbfounded and looking lost, the three stand around while the upset townsfolk continue to disappear into the surroundings... searching and yelling Misty's name. After about fifteen minutes of silence, Chloe decides John would be upset at them for worrying more about him than Misty. Convinced the girl will be found alive and lost somewhere, Chloe feels like she has to do something. She easily talks Steven into staying in wait for the Hounds brothers while she and his father, Mr. Smith, join the search.

First, they make their way down the road toward the store. Their plan is to start there and then move slowly in the direction of the

Crawl residence. According to Mr. Crawl she had walked to the store in the late afternoon for wheat and flour, and never returned. Mr. Smith remembers her leaving the store before six. No one in the entire town could recall seeing her after that point. Chloe's convinced they can track her from the store into the woods where she would be lost and scared but completely unharmed.

Chloe is headstrong and determined to find Misty. Then, once she's found, Chloe intends to beat the crap out of her for being so stupid and putting Michael and John through the violence that they're most likely having to endure. She's more upset at Misty than concerned, which she will soon come to regret. Fearless and angry, Chloe circles the store looking for any footprints she thinks might belong to Misty. Mr. Smith slowly follows behind her, pretending to look at the ground. Though, he appears more lost than helpful.

"Here, these ones must be hers. These prints are fairly large and of a woman's shoe," Chloe observes.

They follow the prints a few yards down the side of the street until they somehow disappear.

"What the hell? This makes no sense," mumbles Chloe.

In place of the woman's shoe prints are now those of a large man. The new prints disappear into the woods and vanish. With all of the deadfall, weeds, leaves and sticks, Chloe and Mr. Smith are unable to pick the tracks back up.

"It makes no sense," Chloe repeats.

"There's gotta be somethin' here we're missin'," she adds. "Look in the trees and weeds too, Mr. Smith. Maybe there's somethin' here that can help us out. All those idiots yellin' and wanderin' 'round are doin' no good at all! Just ruinin' any clues that might help us find her. A bunch of redneck hillbilly idiots!" Chloe rants.

Mr. Smith just smirks at her remarks, and continues to look at the ground in search. He's trying not to say anything that might set her off, or distract him from his own mission on finding clues.

"There!" Chloe yells.

She runs to a small brush containing a tiny piece of ripped cloth.

It's a torn piece of cotton clothing covered in purple flower print. They conclude it could easily be from Misty's dress. Next to the brush are a few drops of blood and more of the mysterious man's footprints.

A burning tingle works its way up Chloe's body, from her toes, to her belly to the top of her head and out. As she looks at the blood on the ground, Chloe knows every thought she had before was wrong. Something terrible has happened to Misty.

"Oh my God," she manages to spit out.

A never speechless Chloe stands there, utterly silent. Everything around them goes quiet and a cloud of fog forms in her head. She's unable to move or think. She's scared and suddenly grateful that she'd convinced Robert Smith to join her, rather than taking off into the woods all by herself, like she normally would've done... fearless and stupid.

"We'd better go and get the Sheriff," Mr. Smith says as he turns back toward the station.

"Wait for me!"

Chloe turns and jogs to catch him, not wanting to be caught alone. Especially not in a place like this, where who knows what could've happened, just the night before.

"I hope they're done talking to Michael and John. This has got to prove them innocent, right?" Chloe asks more to herself than to him. "Do you think Misty's dead?" she adds.

"I don't really know what to think about anything."

Mr. Smith keeps his eyes on the ground in front of him as they work their way back. He chews his bottom lip in contemplation, like he's confused, yet the burning of his eyes make him look as angry as a storm of bees. Chloe can't tell which emotion is more prominent, and the whole vibe is a little disturbing. She shakes the questions of Mr. Smith out of her head. *I'm sure he is just as concerned as everyone else*, she convinces herself.

Walking next to Mr. Smith to the jailhouse is suddenly uncomfortable and nerve racking. Chloe doesn't feel safe at all, and she can't wait to get to Michael. Staying by his side, until this whole mess is straightened out, is exactly what she intends to do. Maybe she can even convince him to break from this mess all together and go back for the bear they'd taken out last night. The thought is comforting, although a part of her knows it'll never happen. That carcass is as good as spoiled.

"There you are," says Steven as he runs to their side. "They still haven't come out and it's been way too quiet. I hope they're okay in there."

Steven's eyes are wide, and he fiddles with his fingernails.

"I wonder if we should go in?" Chloe croaks.

"Dad, are you okay?" Steven asks. "You look upset."

Steven hasn't seen this look on his father's face since the summer before when he was caught sneaking out of the house at night, about to steal the car. They'd done it several times over a two-month time frame. They'd pop the car in neutral and push it until they were out of hearing range, and then jump in and joy-ride all over the county. They'd made a ridiculous amount of money betting on Michael's fighting that summer.

Steven's father usually slept like the dead, but the night they got caught was different. Mr. Smith had been on edge that entire week and had drank an unusual amount of whiskey. He apparently wasn't as passed out as they'd expected. He caught Steven jumping out of the window, before he even had a chance to make it to the driveway. Mr. Smith whipped him good with a belt and sat up all night next to his room to make sure he didn't try to get away again.

The familiar look in Steven's father's eyes sends a white-hot chill completely down his spine. He knows instantly to back off and keep his mouth shut.

"Well, I'm goin' in." Chloe says.

She holds her head as high as possible by lengthening her neck, and straightens her back. Mentally, she tries to harden herself to whatever she might find when she walks through the door. She's also trying to look tough to Steven and his father. Practically everyone from town is out searching, there's no-one in sight. *If this pansy ass Smith family doesn't have what it takes, then I guess I'll have to do it myself,* she thinks. Chloe storms up to the door and pounds her fist against the old rickety wood.

"Put your pants on boys, I'm comin' in whether you like it or not," she shouts.

When she slams her body against the door it swings open with a *creek*. The old hinges barely hold the door in place, so it isn't hard to push it open. Chloe is by no means prepared for what she finds inside.

Both the Hounds brothers are unconscious and handcuffed onto a horizontal bar across the back of the room. Blood drips from each of their noses and some from John's ear. Michael's left eye is swollen shut, and one entire side of his face is black and blue. John's bottom lip is torn right down the center. Chloe can't tell if the majority of the blood is coming from his lip or his nose.

"Oh my god, what did they do to you?" She gasps.

Her feet are glued to the cracked wooden floor as she absorbs the gruesome seen before her. A single tear runs down her cheek.

The sound of Sheriff Black behind her brings bumps to Chloe's arms and the back of her neck. "Awww, there you are," he growls. "You know, both of these scrapping young men refused to scream or speak, because they knew you'd be standing outside waiting."

"Yeah," Deputy Evan chimes in with a chuckle. "The big one even told his weakling brother to stay quiet, to save you a beating right along with them."

"Your scrawny little ass must have quite the pull on these two," says the Sheriff. "Now, if you don't mind, we have a couple other drifters tied to a chair in the other room that we need to attend to."

Both men laugh and saunter off. They seem to be more concerned about the torture they have an opportunity to inflict than they do about finding Misty.

"Wait," Chloe finally finds her voice. "I found something."

"What do you mean 'something'?" asks Deputy Evan.

Again, she straightens her back and holds her head high. She swallows the tears, not giving them a chance to burst through. After coughing out the lump in her throat, she looks up to make eye contact with the Sheriff. No longer is she afraid of this cruel old man and his smelly sidekick. Chloe knows that she's outsmarted them, and has the first lead to finding Misty. She knows she's played her part while these two have done nothing but make more trouble for themselves and the town.

"Go out and ask Robert Smith, he was with me when I found it," she demands. "Now, if you don't mind letting my innocent friends go?"

Chloe stands with her arms folded. The door is still wide open, allowing Steven and his father to hear the entire conversation.

Chloe is proud of herself for her strength, composure, and courage. The Sheriff saunters toward the boys, and with a few loud clicks from a turn of a key, their cuffs loosen. The Hounds brothers tumble to the floor in giant heaps of blood and spit. Chloe races to catch them.

The Sheriff and Deputy walk out the door, right to Mr. Smith. Chloe acts fast, and rips the bottom half of her shirt to use as a cleansing cloth, dabbing at the wounds on each boys' faces. There's a warm cup of water sitting on a small desk in the corner, next to a newspaper and bottle of ink. She uses the water sparingly to wipe off Michael's eye, as well as John's ear and lip.

"I'm so sorry they did this to you," Chloe whispers as the boys stir, slowly regaining consciousness.

Steven hesitantly moves into the station, leaving his father to handle the Sheriff. He helps Chloe get them to their feet. He forces himself between the two of them with an arm under each of their pits. Steven half carries and half steadies them as they scurry out of the dark room and into the fresh air and sunlight of outside. Steven knows the owner's wife will be there in place of his father. She'll surely be passing out supplies and bullets to help in the aid of the search. They decide that it'll be the best place to tend to the Hounds boys' wounds. With Steven's father working there for years, they'll be able to put all of the first aid supplies on his personal tab.

"I hope your dad can get the Sheriff back to the place we found Misty's clothes and blood before that creep who took her can get rid of the evidence."

Chloe tells Steven as they struggle to get the heavy young men to the store. John winces at the new information, unable to speak in response.

"Your dad didn't seem very happy when we found it. He must be pretty upset at the guy who took her," she adds.

"Yeah he wouldn't talk about it or tell me anything when you went into the jailhouse either," Steven replies.

He can't seem to get the look on his father's face out of his head. Even while carrying his bloodied friends, that look is stuck. It was an unfocused look of hate and plotting. It seems to Steven that his father is hiding something. *Most likely thinking about what he would do to the guy who took her, I'd hate to be anyone who crossed my father,* Steven thinks.

He knows how painful the sting of his father's whip can be, as well as the impact of his fists. Steven knows that crazy look in his father's eye well, and knows he doesn't want to be anywhere around if he snaps. Mr. Smith is a very tall man. He is covered in freckles, and has an abnormally long arm span. He is big boned with hardly any fat and an enormous frame. Though he works in a store and is usually a cheerful and sociable man, he has a dark side... very dark. Few people around have seen this side of Mr. Smith, and are better off for it.

Steven's mother has always seemed to have a strange fear of Steven's father. She has often told him, "Me and your father had our differences, but he is a good dad. Just don't cross him, Son."

These were her exact words on several occasions. She'd cry for days and even pray an unusual amount, for about a week before it was time for Steven to stay with his dad in the summers. Steven knows that any mother would have a hard time saying goodbye to her son for such long lengths of time. He usually just rolls his eyes and tells her that he'll be just fine.

Now, as Steven walks to the store he's spent so much time in over the years, he feels like an outsider. He can't place why he has such a strange knot in his stomach. The thought of his mother's fear and the rage in his father's eyes has his mind wandering. He knows that for some reason, he and his father are out of place in this town. There's something not quite whole. Like a missing piece of a jigsaw puzzle, right smack in the middle. He can't push the loneliness he feels for his mother out of his chest. All Steven wants at this very moment is to be home. In his real home, with his mom where he's comfortable and safe.

"Are you okay, Red?" Michael stutters through a bloodied mouth.

Every step they take is a battle.

"Yeah, I'm just a little freaked out, that's all. You worry about yourself right now."

The four stumble into the store and nearly collapse onto the floor. A few older women run to their aide.

"Oh, dear Lord," one woman gasps. "We'll get some alcohol, gauze, and a few blankets. You kids get them to the beds in the back, so that we get them cleaned up and taken care of as fast as possible."

The woman scurries from shelf to shelf. She's slim with short dark hair, and a solid green dress. She moves with speed and efficiency. Michael is instantly relieved to have such a lady there to help them. He thinks she looks familiar, like he's seen her talking to his mother from time to time, but his vision is blurry. He's having a hard time concentrating on anything aside from the pain in his ribs.

Soon, Michael looks up at Chloe from the hard mattress in the dark and damp back room of the store. He gives his best effort to flash her a smile.

"So, how about that bear?" he asks in a dry and raspy voice.

"Only you would bring up a dead animal at a time like this." She forces one short huff of a giggle. "I'll bet some old farmer found it while they were searching, and claimed it was himself who killed it."

Chloe can't help but picture a few old men standing around the carcass they'd left in the dark the night before. They'd be looking at the size of its paws and teeth. They'd be making up their story as they took responsibility for being the mightiest hunters around. Chloe rolls her eyes and shakes her head at the thought, chuckling to herself over the image.

"You know, if all this crap didn't happen this morning, we could be getting enough supplies at the market to feed your family for the next month. Do you want me to go check on your mom, or do you want me to wait here with you?"

Chloe hasn't forgotten about Mrs. Hounds sitting alone at home with no protection, weak and sick with a possible killer on the loose.

Panic runs through Michael's veins as the same thought crosses his mind.

"Oh my God, my mom is all by herself and..."

He stops mid- sentence, not wanting to imagine what could possibly be going on at his house.

"Chloe, you have to make sure she's okay, but you can't go alone."

Michael's voice comes out raspy and afraid. The rusty taste of blood in the back of his throat grows to an unbearable measure. Michael is unable to swallow with the pain in his neck and chest. He rolls to his side and spits the accumulating blood from his mouth into a large bowl setting next to his bed. John is in a bed a few feet away, passed out. He's unable to maintain consciousness for more than a few minutes at a time. Clearly, John took the worst of the beatings.

"Have Steven go with you to check on my mom."

Michael winces with every word. He leans his head back on the soft clean pillow. As soon as his eyes close, the memory of the Sheriff's blows to John's hands and feet with a cane are front and center. John was unable to answer or defend himself before each hit made contact with his bones. The Sheriff wasn't interested in answers, he was only interested in the chance to unleash his own personal frustration.

Deputy Evan doesn't have the same kind of pent up anger that the Sheriff does. He's merely a nasty man with a cold heart, and nothing more. Deputy Evan enjoys seeing pain inflicted on people. He likes the way it makes him feel. The power, like he's in charge. He loves the God-like spiritual lift that comes with holding a man's life in his hands.

Michael kept his mouth shut for Chloe and Steven's sake, while he watched his brother take the worst of it. He hung there by his arms, handcuffed to the pole, basically just waiting for his turn. Luckily, the first hit to the back of the head knocked him out, so he didn't feel the pain until after he woke up. Chloe's angel face, and her gentle hands dabbing him down with a wet piece of cloth is really all he can remember.

The Sheriff knows from experience that Michael will always find a way to fight back... unless he is unconscious. His goal was to torture Michael with the beating he gave to his brother first, and then the pain he'd feel when he awoke. His plot worked and Michael lay there now with nothing but pain and the memories of his brother's torture.

"Mrs. Victor is here with her car, so we can get to your house a little faster with her help."

"Thank you, Chloe." Michael whispers.

He stares at her as she stands in the doorway. The weight of a rock presses down on his chest.

"I love you," he cracks, with a tear rolling down his cheek.

The door frame supports Chloe's weight as the leans against it. Her knees are weak, and her breath is shallow.

"I love you too," she breathes, hardly even a whisper.

"Wait." Michael stops her before she's completely out the door. "Please Chloe, just be careful... come back to me."

Chloe walks out the door holding her breath, and refuses to look back. She can't bear to see the vulnerable look of pain on Michael's bruised and swelling face. All she wants to do is rush back to his side and hold him and comfort him until he falls asleep. She knows without a doubt that if she turns around now, then she'll never be able to pry herself back out of the room. The bleeding heart in

Chloe's chest wants her to collapse at his side, but the practical side of her knows that she has to be strong... for both of the Hounds brothers.

After making a vow to herself to help find Misty and bring her back to John, Chloe can't let herself give up. She has to hold herself together now more than ever. Chloe understands that her entire life with the Hounds family depends on how this day will play out. The rest of her life will be shaped and molded from this very day. Michael slowly drifts into unconsciousness as he prays to God to watch over his mom, Chloe, and his brother.

Steven climbs into the front seat of Mrs. Victor's pickup, with a shotgun gripped tightly in his fingers. Mrs. Victor drives and Chloe sits anxiously in the back. They all keep a close eye out for anything out of the ordinary. Their nerves and emotions are itching under the surface.

Mrs. Victor's glad to help in any way she can. She's a distant cousin to Mr. Crawl and more like an Aunt to Misty than anyone else around. They are a fairly close family and Mrs. Victor seems to be holding herself together very well, given the situation. She went straight to the store after dropping Michael and Mr. Crawl off at the Jail house earlier that morning. She knew that anyone with new information would end up in the store before going anywhere else. The store is a place of contact and familiarity to all the townsfolk, and a center point for the search.

Mrs. Victor knew she'd be of better use helping those who came into the store, than she would be at home. She also doesn't want to be caught in the woods by herself while searching if there really is some sort of psycho on the loose. Giving Steven and Chloe a ride to the Hounds residence gives her a feeling of usefulness, and a minute to escape the stress of the store and catch her breath. The ride is short and silent.

"I'm coming in with the two of you, if you don't mind" Mrs. Victor says as they pull up to the house. "I'm not very comfortable waiting outside all alone."

With a heavy head, she drops her chin to her chest in shame. She doesn't know why, but it makes her feel guilty. Like a coward, to be scared of solitude.

"Yes, of course." Steven says. "You're more than welcome to come in. We wouldn't have it any other way, Ma'am."

Chloe climbs out first, lost in her own thoughts. She walks up to the door, scared and exhausted. She enters the home first to see Mrs. Hounds pulling herself up to a seated position. Mrs. Hounds is weak and holding a handkerchief, embroidered in blue flowers around the edges, but stained with blood. Slowly dying of tuberculosis, Mrs. Hounds has been unable to speak above a whisper, or eat much for the last several months.

Despite the fact that she's always in pain and coughing blood every day, she's remained positive. She's convinced that if she keeps a good attitude then God may eventually cure her. The vision of Chloe dragging her feet through the door, and without her boys close in tow, causes the corners of her face to drop with worry.

"Is everything okay honey?" Her scratchy voice is hardly audible. "I heard the bells a few hours back and everyone was gone."

Steven and Mrs. Victor follow Chloe into the home, and Mrs. Hounds' stomach churns. Panic settles in her core.

"Where are my sons?"

Mrs. Victor eases herself slowly onto the couch next to her, and begins explaining details of Misty's disappearance. All the while Chloe and Steven fetch a drink of water and some bread in milk with ginger, to ease and settle Mrs. Hound's stomach. They work together in silence while listening in on Mrs. Victor's explanation to Mrs. Hounds. The details of the search and of the evidence that Chloe and Mr. Smith had found on the outskirts of town linger in the air like a plague.

The extremity of the interrogation inflicted on Michael and John are excluded. Soon, the four are all gathered together on the worn-down furniture in the dimly lit room. They sugar coat details, stating that the boys were merely questioned and are now at the store helping the townsfolk.

Mrs. Hounds can tell by the look on their faces that her boys are in worse shape than they're letting on. Michael's previous experience with Sheriff Black is a strong testament that he wouldn't be so easy on either of them in a full-on interrogation. She tries to swallow the excruciating lump in the back of her throat. Mrs. Hounds knows she'll find out soon enough, the severity of the shape of her boys' well-being.

Steven offers to stay with Mrs. Hounds while Mrs. Victor and Chloe embark on rallying up the other women nearby. Upon the town's orders to stay indoors with their children, they decide a group setting may be best.

Chloe and Mrs. Victor have no trouble convincing the women who are spread out and alone to rally together at the Hounds' residence, especially while they have a ride to get there. Mrs. Hounds is in no shape to leave her home, so they're determined to bring help to her. It doesn't take them long to round up five women with their children.

They intend to stay there, and take care of one another until Misty is found. After that, their families will return to the comfort of their own homes. They're a strong and determined bunch of women and should have no trouble fending off any intruders if they work together. It brings Mrs. Victor, Chloe and Steven comfort as they make their way back to town. An anchored feel of accomplishment takes place, and is topped off with a layer of safe-keeping.

Michael and John are sitting up and talking by the time they return to the tiny room in the back of the store. Sore, and with slow movements, they've both regained full consciousness, and are ready to do whatever they're physically capable of. Given the broken ribs and blurred sight, what they're able to do will surely be limited. But they're ready and willing nonetheless.

John's feet are swollen, and there are sure to be at least couple of broken bones peppered throughout his body. Its unbearable for him to stand for long, or to walk very far. While waiting for Steven and Chloe, John had told Michael how he felt about Misty, and that he'd suffer through the pain until she's found.

"God, I'm useless," John moans in frustration as he sits back down after a few moments of standing by his bed. "How am I supposed to find her, if I can't even walk the distance of the store?"

He drops his head into his hands, trying to hold back the frustration that's bubbling inside. He's completely broken hearted.

"All I'm good for now is making it even harder for her to be found, because I have to be taken care of too."

John is very hard on himself, a little too much so. The time is rolling into mid-afternoon and there's still no sign of misty. The only thing anyone has found to give some kind of lead, is the torn cloth that Chloe came across a couple of hours ago. Mr. Smith and Sheriff Black still haven't returned and there's been no word on the progress of the search.

"Has he been like this the whole time we've been gone?" Steven asks Michael under his breath.

"Yes," Michael mumbles.

"Well, we'd better get out there then," says Chloe steadily. "You know if there was any kind of blood trail that might lead to Misty, them damned old jackasses called the law is gunna' to ruin it. Stompin' 'round on all the evidence."

She stops mid-sentence, looking over at John. Chloe instantly realizes that she's said too much, and everything else that comes out of her mouth is only going to cause him more pain.

"Sorry John. Try to get some rest," she mumbles, before dropping her head and spinning on her heels for the door.

Steven and Michael follow out close behind her, leaving John to stew, and hopefully heal some. They move slowly to the front of the store, out of ear range from John before they begin to formulate a plot.

"I think we should start where you found that cloth with my dad, and try to track her ourselves," declares Steven.

"Me too," Michael agrees. "And, I say even if we see or find anything, we don't let anyone in on it until we get to Misty."

Chloe is clearly irritated at Michael. She narrows her eyes at him, and throws a palm to her hip.

"I think you should stay here and rest with your brother."

It only takes a moment for that irritation to melt. She looks closely at the blood on Michael's lip, blaming herself for the swelling in his face, along with the still forming bruises down his neck and shoulders. If he only would've yelled or made a sound, then she and Steven could've helped them out.

"Don't be stupid Chloe, you know I can't just sit here helpless while you guys are out searching. I can walk just fine. It's all in my ribs and face."

Every time Michael moves the pain snakes through his body. But he'll never let Chloe know exactly how much pain he's in. As for now, he silently thanks the powers that be, for her to be safe and by his side. There's no way he's going to let her go anywhere without him.

"Besides Chloe, I'm not letting you out of my sight... like ever."

He glances out the corner of his eye at her pinkened cheeks. Only this time he isn't joking around with his suggestive comments just to see her squirm. This time, he means every word he says to her, and can feel the raw truth in it from deep in the bottom of his stomach. Something strange is going on here, dangerously so. Michael knows that he'd never forgive himself if anything were to happen to Chloe.

CHAPTER FIVE

S heriff Black and Deputy Evan follow Robert Smith, out past the store and down the road. Mr. Smith shows them the footprints that appear to be of a woman's shoe, and how they disappear into the woods. He shows them how the large man's footprints take the place of that first set, they presumed to belong to Misty. It's a little harder this second time around, to tell what tracks may actually belong to whom, since he and Chloe have also walked through the area. Now, with the Sheriff and the Deputies' tracks alongside the rest, everyone's tracks seem to blend together. As they enter the woods to look at the flower print torn cloth and the blood on the ground, the Sheriff stops in his tracks.

"Deputy Evan, you had better stay in town. Go on back to the jail house in case anything else comes up," the Sheriff demands.

"But, but, but." The Deputy stutters, shocked and very clearly unhappy about Sheriff Black's orders. "Why can't I see what's in the woods, too?" He whines.

Deputy Evan is of no help at all, as usual. He's only curious and eager to witness what shape they'd find the young girl in and the reaction it would have on Sheriff Black.

"Just go Evan. You're stinkin' up the crime scene anyway," Sheriff Black mumbles in a low gruff voice.

He then turns his attention to Mr. Smith, completely careless to the Deputy or to his reaction to the rejection.

"Well, lead the way, Big Red."

With that, they disappear into the woods and Deputy Evan turns back toward the jailhouse. He mumbles and kicks his awkwardly large feet, while slowly moping his way in the opposite direction to the other two. Deputy Evan has been excited all morning. He has fed off the chaos and enjoyed inflicting pain.

He's not happy about being pushed out of the first hand search. The Deputy knows that if any other information comes up, the townsfolk likely won't come to him at the jailhouse, not without the Sheriff there. They'd be much more likely to go to the store and deal with the situation amongst each other. He'd be excluded from everything to do with the search from here on out.

On the other hand, Deputy Evan also realizes that he can't just abandon his post. He has to be at the jailhouse, in case any other men of the law from surrounding counties show up. They sent word out of the search, so such a scenario isn't exactly out of the question.

There's also a matter of the two drifters, waiting behind... tied up and hidden from the public. A slow grin melts over Evan's face like butter, and his steps grow a little quicker as he contemplates what may be in store for them. With Sheriff Black not around to take charge and inflict the first blow, he'd be able to deal with them in whatever ruthless way he sees fit.

Robert and Sheriff Black walk up to the brush containing the cloth, it's still the same way Chloe had left it.

"There it is."

Mr. Smith points a stiff finger at the shrubbery before he looks over at the Sheriff. The skin of his forehead is pinched in anger. The Sheriff glances back at Robert, confused and a bit taken back by the contorted look on his face. Sheriff Black is the first to break the eye contact, along with the unspoken tension slowly rising between them.

"Yep, sure does look suspicious. It has to belong to the girl, there's no other excuse for the blood."

Sheriff Black states the obvious while he stares at the evidence in front of him. He would never admit it out loud, but he doesn't have a clue as to what the next move should be.

"I guess we should keep looking around for any more blood," he finally mumbles.

Mr. Smith's eyes do a full circle. He taps his foot, irritated at Sheriff Black, and waits for him to come up with some sort of game plan. With nervous hands grabbing at his belt buckle, Mr. Smith glares at the Sheriff. After a few meaningless and wasteful moments of walking around aimlessly, he decides to take matters into his own hands.

"I'm going to find a few more men to help us track the blood, just in case we need help when we find her."

"That's probably a good idea, Robert."

Sheriff Black nods and scratches at his chin. While wandering around the likely crime scene, the Sheriff tries wrapping his mind around why Mr. Smith had such a hostile look in his eyes. It seemed almost like he was angry at the fact they were looking at the torn cloth at all. *Strange behavior*, he thinks. Any of the other townsmen would be in a hurry to get to Misty, and not in a hurry to leave. What a strange man indeed.

"Well, I suppose I'd better get onto some kind of blood trail here," the Sheriff says to himself.

He looks around the ground and bushes until he spots another drop, and then another, and then another. It doesn't take long for the small drops to grow bigger and bigger. What starts as the size of a pin head every few feet, progresses into what looks like cups full of scarlet fluid, dumped in the mud and muck.

The Sheriff debates on whether to keep going on his own, or to wait for help in the case of a possible ambush. He bats back and forth in his mind until he ultimately decides that the sooner he gets to the girl, the more likely he is to save her in the unlikely event she's still alive. He fires a couple rounds from his always loaded revolver into the air, hoping that if there are any other search parties near enough to hear it, they'd start to move in his direction.

He stacks a few logs and branches in strange places, hoping to leave some kind of a trail of his own, just in case the blood is passed over. *Surely, someone around this hell hole will be smart enough to find and follow this many clues,* he thinks. On edge and very cautiously, the Sheriff moves along the blood trail on the ground at a snail's pace. He takes his time, assuming that Mr. Smith has been able to find some kind of backup. Of course, Mr. Smith is yet to catch back up. Depending entirely on his help is out of the question.

The further Sheriff Black moves into the woods, the more on edge he becomes. Every little crack of a stick under his feet causes his heart to thump harder. He continues to fire an occasional round, crossing his fingers that it's heard. Each time, he quickly reloads, keeping his weapon fully loaded. He only has enough extra ammunition in his pocket to reload his old six shooter two more times. *Damned ol' revolver misfires too much as it is,* the Sheriff thinks, deciding it best to save what's left for when he finds whatever is actually at the end of this blood trail.

The crusted, scarlet puddles continue to thicken. He wonders if there's any way possible for the bleeder to actually be alive by the time he reaches its culprit. It's got to be Misty. There are no animal tracks, only the same prints of the large man's boot and occasional drag marks in the dirt. Time is also an issue, of that the Sheriff is acutely aware. Since Misty went missing the night before, and it is now in the mid-afternoon, whatever he's bound to find at the end of this trail isn't going to be pretty.

The Sheriff wonders if anyone actually heard his shots, or if he'd be on his own from here on out. He tightens his grip on the stock of his shooter, and makes a very unsuccessful effort to slow his breath and the pounding of his heart.

Before the Sheriff knows it, he's a couple miles into the woods, where a long tree line opens up into a small round clearing. The blood trail stops and there are mounds of soft dirt, moved around. The entire flat has clearly been dug in several places. The ground's surface is disturbed in every direction, with dirt swirled in places and rocks stacked in others. Sheriff Black picks up a large stick and starts poking around at the dirt with it. He's not sure where to start, or what to do. He has no shovel and no clue.

He cusses at himself under his breath the whole time he scrapes at the ground with his stick. Thirst paws at the back of his throat, as the heat of the sun beats down on his shoulders. The Sheriff usually has a canteen on his belt, but in the chaos of the day he hadn't even thought to grab it as he walked away from the jailhouse behind Robert Smith. Suddenly, there's a rustle in the trees behind him. He spins on his heels to face the sound, and quickly draws his gun.

"Hold it right there and say your name," Sheriff Black yells into the tree line.

"Don't shoot!" A deep scratchy voice shouts back at him. "We're part of the search. We heard shots and moved toward them as fast as we could."

Two men come into sight holding their rifles, one with a lantern and rope, the other with a shovel. Sheriff Black sighs a breath of relief, recognizing their faces as they approach. They're cousins who share a farm on the far south fields outside of town, both are very large and very quiet men. They rarely come into town and have never caused any trouble. Aside from chasing off trespassers and thieves from their property, these men are hardly ever seen or heard from. The Sheriff can't seem to recall their first names, only that they belong to the Trudge family. He knows there are several children in the family, and more than a couple wives on their farm. The town keeps a tight lip about the Trudge lifestyle, and in turn they all pretty much mind their own business.

"I sure am glad for the help boys, I don't think I could do much more digging with this here stick," says Sheriff Black.

"Do you think it's a grave?" asks the larger of the two Trudge men.

"Nawh, this is just a distraction," says the other, in a thick southern accent. "See over there a bit further? The grounds' been swiped aroun' the top and not dug. See how the ground' is all swirly? This here where your diggin', Sheriff, jus' had dirt threw on top a' the blood. There aint nothin' buried here."

The man speaks with confidence, and it sends a chill through the Sheriff's bones. His southern accent is the deepest Sheriff Black has ever heard.

"Well, ain't you never buried nothin'?" The man rolls his eyes at the blank look on the Sheriff's face and continues. "When you dig a hole you gotta throw 'ur dirt somewhar'. 'Ur diggin' in the wrong place."

The large middle aged farmer walks a few yards over and jams his shovel into the ground. After a couple of shovels full of fresh ground, there's a loud *thud* that comes from the ground.

"Now, what 'n Sam's hell is 'dis?"

The farmer mumbles, and continues to dig around and uncover a wooden plank. It has hinges on one side and a handle on the other. Apparently, the man has exposed a small 'lift from the ground' door of some sort. It looks to the Sheriff like an access door to an old storm shelter.

"There must be some kinda' room or bunker down yonder," says the larger man, standing post with his rifle. "After you, Sheriff," he continues, while looking over his shoulder at Sheriff Black with a daring smirk.

The smaller of the two farmers tosses his shovel a few yards over his shoulder before lifting the door. The hinges sound an eerie *squeak* as it rises from the ground. The only thing visible is an old ladder that drops down into the dark lair.

Cautiously, the men lower themselves in. The inside of the bunker is damp and dark. A few three by fours are leaning against the walls of the hole, holding up the thin wooden roof no doubt. There's no telling how long this bunker's been here hidden, just over a couple miles out of town. The three men stand at the base of the ladder, each one a little too nervous to go any further into the dark. They can't see more than a couple of inches in front of them, but the ground is sticky and the odor is unbearable.

"How the hell hasn't this place been found?" Questions one of the young farmers.

"We need more light," says the other. "Better get out, and get that lantern goin', 'fore we go pokin' 'round even more in the dark."

Sheriff Black nods to himself, agreeing quietly with the Trudge men. He's the first man out of the bunker, and sets to work lighting the lantern.

"Maybe one of us should stay out here, you know, in case anyone else shows up. I don't know 'bout you two, but I don't wanna' to be locked down there if the owner of this place finds us here."

"You're right cousin, it wouldn't take much if we were all down there for 'em to lock us in. I guess since you dug the hole, I'd better be the one who goes. Fair 'n all."

The larger of the two Trudge men climbs down the ladder before reaching up for the lantern. Sheriff Black hands it down, then follows behind. The room isn't big, and now with a light inside they can see everything. It's gruesome and overwhelming, even for the evil old Sheriff who is clearly no stranger to blood. The young farmer holding the light, bends at the waist to throw up before he can even take a step toward Misty's body. It's been cut into several pieces, and lain out in the single room dirt bunker... as if on display. The smell is more than his stomach can withstand.

There are also remains of at least one other victim from years before, possibly more. Old, meatless bones are littered around the edges of the space.

"I wonder who those belong to?" The Sheriff finally finds his voice. "What the hell are we to do with this mess?"

Before a second round of vomit can escape the farmer, they turn around and yet again make the climb back up the ladder. They breathe in the fresh mountain air, as if their lives depend on it.

"Well, what was down there, cousin?" asks the Trudge man, waiting outside.

The shirtless farmer collapses to the ground next to a tree, speechless and unable to explain the gruesome details of the bunker.

He stutters, "I... I... we... she..."

The Sheriff is able to speak a little more steadily, yet doesn't quite know what to say.

"She is in pieces," he replies. "We're gunna' have to call in more law and a box to carry her out in. Maybe you boys should stay here and make sure no one else goes into that hole," he adds.

The Sheriff rushes off with a defeated chin to his chest. He's lost in his own head as he wanders away from the other two men. They silently agree and begin to gather firewood. No further words are exchanged with the Sheriff.

"You're gunna' have to tell me what you saw down there, cousin." Declares the farmer as the Sheriff makes his way out of sight. "You're white as a ghost and I know that was you I heard blowin' chunks."

He won't let up until he has an idea of the contents in the hole he was guarding with his life.

"If I'm gunna' sit here waiting, ready to shoot anyone who walks up, you better be sharin' the details," he continues to push.

"I aint never saw nothin' like that," The larger man stammers. "She, she, she was sawed into pe... pe... pieces. There is so much blood. It was like standing in a, a, a, a lake. Her head is sitting in the corner with her hair all cut off... Even her, her, her feet are missin' the toes."

He has a blank, sick, look on his face while describing the horror. He's unable to blink or take a breath. He stammers his speech and stumbles over his words. This man would be changed forever and unable to sleep for years to come. No other words are exchanged between the two cousins for several minutes. They sit there on post speechless, petrified, and utterly disgusted.

CHAPTER SIX

Chloe and Steven help Michael through the woods, following the same blood trail Sheriff Black was just on not too long ago. They see the logs and branches he'd moved around.

"I'm surprised that dumbass actually has enough brains to leave any kind of clues." Steven says as they move into the unknown.

Chloe squints into the bushes. "Well, well, if it isn't Sheriff Black. Did you find anything?" She asks.

Sheriff Black stares wide-eyed at the three for a few seconds before answering. A part of him is surprised that Michael is out and about, not so long after the beating that was handed to him. Michael stiffens his back until it's straight as an arrow, as to not show how much pain he's actually in. He makes eye contact with Sheriff Black, making it a point not to look away. Michael refuses to show any weakness.

Sheriff Black is still very shaken and disturbed. With the image of Misty, dismembered in that hole, he brushes off Michael's quiet defiance. The Sheriff's skin is pale and clammy, it looks like he's seen a ghost. Each breath taken in is shallow, and he can't do much aside from stare at the three young teens with confusion and regret.

For the first time in Sheriff Black's life, he actually feels bad about ruthlessly beating a man during interrogation. He looks closely at Michael's swollen eye and lip. The bruises are forming down his neck and shoulders, and his arm is clutching at his ribs.

Sheriff Black gives his own family and loved ones a quick thought. He also ponders on all of the 'what if's', much like John had before. *What if Misty was one of my own? What if he kills anyone else in my town? What if this man has been arrested and in my jailhouse and I let him go? What if I could have saved her, had I not been interrogating the Hounds boys for the duration of the morning?*

The Sheriff is sick and a part of him is grateful that he hadn't eaten much that morning. Sheriff Black couldn't tell why he was yet to puke, much like the farmer who stood next to him in the bunker.

"Well, did you?" Steven asks again.

"Huh?"

He's wading through the fog of his thoughts, trying to remember the question they asked in the first place.

Steven repeats, "Did you find anything?"

He finally forms words. "Yes, and you kids don't want to see it. Besides, I don't want anyone else poking around the crime scene until we can get some back up."

"Well, at least tell us if she is alive or dead," demands Michael, thinking that it's the least he can do.

"She is dead," Sheriff Black breathes, hardly a whisper. "And, you had probably better get home to your families until we can figure it all out. I don't think it best to have all these people spread out in the woods with a killer of this nature around."

The Sheriff ducks around them, and continues on his walk back to the jailhouse where he'd have a message sent to all of the surrounding counties yet again. This time, including details of Misty's body and a plea for help. Sheriff Black knows it'll surely be a long and very tragic summer for his town.

In light of the day's events, the Sheriff has an epiphany of self. He swears to himself that he would fire Deputy Evan and find an honest

Deputy who knows the law and will fight to help save their town, rather than help him to run it down and stink it up. He had put in a replacement request months ago, but he never found anyone to fill the Deputy shoes, and never pushed the matter any further.

Sheriff Black knows the teens won't turn around and go home, they're far too stubborn. But, at the same time, he's too drained to fight them. Before he's completely out of their sight he turns around and hollers back to them.

"Hey, Michael Hounds," he shouts just loud enough to be heard. "It will never happen again."

He leaves the statement in the air, lingering, then spins back around and keeps on walking back to the jailhouse.

A chill of relief crawls through Michael's veins. He knows the Sheriff is talking about the events that happened in the jailhouse today. Michael could see the pain and regret in Sheriff Black's face. *Whatever he found out there must be truly terrible to make such a nasty man have a change of heart*, he thought.

"I don't buy it," whispers Steven. "He is a liar, I will never believe a word that comes out of that man's mouth."

Steven is disgusted by the Sheriff and always has been. So far, he has been lucky and avoided any type of confrontation with the man. Every other time that Michael or John have crossed the Sheriff, Steven wasn't in town. Steven had always been secretly grateful he wasn't ever around when Michael had been arrested. Even though he has bragged and boasted about what he would have done to the Sheriff and Deputy had he been around, everyone knows that Steven is all talk. He's been in several fights, but when it comes to the law, he's merely a young, frightened boy.

"I ain't goin' home just yet," says Chloe. "I'm gunna' go see what's got that ugly old man all worked up." Her attention is turned back to the blood trail on the ground. "I'm gunna' wanna' know what to tell John when we get back. I know he wouldn't want us to turn around and run away with our tails between our legs like a couple a whipped dogs."

Chloe picks up the pace, leading the way even further into the woods. Michael and Steven follow, each one quiet and utterly lost in their own thoughts while they follow close behind.

Michael declares, "I don't think you're gunna' want to see her body if it's there Chloe. I mean, I know you're tough and all, but I don't want you to have to remember it for the rest of your life. Maybe you should stick behind me and Red, just in case we come across somethin' soon."

Authority and confidence bleeds through Michael's words, though he doesn't completely feel the truth in it. The further they walk, the more excruciating is the pain. It moves from the heels of his feet, through his legs and settles in the whole of his torso.

Chloe stops in her tracks and waits for Michael and Steven to catch up and pass her on the trail. She loves Michael and can tell by the tone of his voice that he isn't playing around. Chloe would do anything he asked of her in that tone of voice. In a way it makes her feel safe and cared for. Slowly, she slips her hand into his, and they lock eyes for a brief moment. A white-hot chill runs down her spine. They may have touched before when brushing past one another, or even wrestling around, but there has never been this drive of emotion between them.

Michael intertwines her fingers even further into his own, and squeezes them tightly. It feels good to admit his love for Chloe, and to feel her body react the way it does when he touches her. His chest is pounding. He thinks about what they might find the further they go into the woods.

He knows that a young girl is dead, and his brother will be heart-broken. He also realizes that whatever Sheriff Black witnessed has somehow changed him from a cruel heartless man into a shell of grief and regret. Michael takes in a deep breath and lets it out slowly. He can smell the smoke of a fire coming out of the trees up ahead of them.

"Wait Red, do you hear that?" He asks while stopping to listen to the voices up ahead.

"Yeah, I do."

Steven too stops in his tracks. He holds his breath and listens. Hesitantly, they decided to keep walking. There are at least two voices ahead, and they sound fairly friendly. Their deep southern accents carry into the woods toward Michael, Steven and Chloe. As they get a little closer to the voices, they decided to make themselves known as not to startle anyone on high alert. No one wants to get shot in the confusion and adrenaline of the day.

"Who is there?" Steven shouts. "Are you a part of the search party?"

"It's Paul and Jerry Trudge." Both men yell back in unison.

Slowly and cautiously, they approach the fire that the farmers have built. They discuss the events of the day and the underground bunker just a few feet away from the flames. The farmers explain to the teens how they'd found it, and exactly what was sitting inside. The color drains from Chloe's face as she listens and stares at the exposed door to the underground room containing the remains of Misty's body.

The smell of the death surrounds them, and it's growing stronger with every breath as they wait for help to come. None of them has any desire to go down the ladder and look inside the room, they just take the farmer's word for it. Paul Trudge is still pale and nauseated, unable to describe many details of what he'd witnessed. He's thrown up a few more times, and is still unable to stop the occasional tears from leaking out the corners of his eyes.

"I wonder how much longer we should stay here and wait for the Sheriff to get help?" speculates the smaller farmer.

Steven speaks up, trying to convince himself of something positive, just as much as he's trying to convince the others.

"I don't think it'll take too much longer. I'm sure he'll be on Ol' Blue this time around and with help. Plus, he'll know exactly where to go."

For some reason, Steven is still internally bothered by the look he'd seen on his father's face. He's distracted and partly consumed by the thought of it. Even with the body of a dead girl in the ground a few feet away, Steven still can't manage to pull his mind from his father.

"Maybe we should go back and let John know Misty is dead," says Chloe, in a cold uncomfortable voice.

"Yeah we probably should," answers Michael.

"You kids go ahead back to town." Paul Trudge speaks up. "There ain't no need for all of us to sit here in this smell."

Jerry Trudge adds, "we was here when she was found, we'll stay here till she's taken care of."

The Trudge cousins are patient and determined, not able to bring themselves to leave the scene, just in case the killer shows up to check on his victim's remains.

Steven decides to stay with the Trudge farmers, assuming that he can be of some some use. Michael and Chloe head back to break the awful news to John. They walk away from the blood trail this time, choosing not to stare at the constant reminder, and make way toward the town on their own. Once they're out of site, Michael stops and grabs Chloe by the waist to pull her under the shade of a tree.

"You know, when I said I love you today it wasn't just because I was hurt. I meant it Chloe, and I mean it now. I've loved you for as long as I can remember. I know I don't have the money you're used to, and I probably never will. But I can take care of you. I'll spend the rest of my life trying to make you happy."

Michael has so many things he wants to tell her. He's been waiting to confess his love and rehearsing the words he'd say to her for years. Michael holds her tight and can feel the energy between them when he speaks. With every word he says there's a new tear streaming down Chloe's face. Michael's lips gently touched Chloe's in their first perfect kiss.

"I love you too, Michael Hounds." She whispers, the very moment their lips part.

A surge of energy passes through her flesh and escapes from her chest. She draws in a deep breath, letting herself feel every inch of his body pressed against hers. She can see the vulnerability in his emerald eyes. She can feel the muscles of his stomach and chest, as they push against her. His arms are wrapped firmly around her waist and back.

Slowly, Michael moves his hand up her back, allowing it to stop at the base of her neck as he kisses her once again. Their second kiss lasts much longer, leaving the taste of it to linger, and their movements to sink into a rhythm all of their own. Chloe has been dreaming of the warmth of Michael's body, more lately than ever, and she's been imagining the taste of his tongue on hers. All the stress on their shoulders fades into the background, if only for a brief moment. The only two people on the planet are Michael Hounds and Chloe Mead.

They lean back to gaze at each other one last time before allowing their bodies to pull away from one another. Knowing that they must return to the tragedy that this strange day has presented, they continued back to town and to the reality hand in hand.

"How are we gunna' tell John about what happened to Misty?" Chloe breaks their comfortable silence. "I just want this whole mess to be over. He never even told her how he felt about her." Chloe is heartbroken for John.

"I don't know. I've never seen him act this way. I guess we'll just have to be honest and tell him everything we've seen and heard."

"You know, Steven's dad was acting really strangely when I found that piece of her dress." Chloe remembers. A chill runs up her spine as she recalls that look in his eyes. "I don't think I've ever been that uncomfortable around him. He was kinda' scary even," she admits.

"I'm sure he was just mad at the killer, Chloe. I don't think anything is wrong with Robert Smith."

Michael isn't paying much attention to her concern, and blows off her worry with a toss of his head.

"I mean it Michael, he was really weird. Do you ever wonder what he was doing with those crossbows, and rope, and all those knives? I mean, he really doesn't seem like the kind of person that would collect that kind of stuff. I never really thought 'bout it till now. And for some reason it keeps crossing my mind. I think we should sneak back into the basement in Steven's house and see what else is in that room."

The more Chloe speaks, the more she convinces herself that Steven's dad has a secret, perhaps even a dark one, and she now has Michael just as curious.

"Okay, we'll go take a look but I don't want Steven or John to know what we're doing."

"Good thinkin'. Maybe we should spend time with John for a while, at least until sometime tomorrow. We have to get him home to rest his feet and hands anyway, and then we could go and look when everything has cooled down in the morning and Mr. Smith is at the store. We could send Steven to go check on John and we'll make a break for the basement."

Chloe formulates her plot aloud, and Michael agrees on it. They set their plan into place, down to the very last detail. If there is anything in that basement, then they surely don't want to be caught looking at it. And, if there's not anything down there, then they don't want to look like they've accused anyone of anything out of the ordinary either.

Michael and Chloe wander back into town just in time to hear the sound of several men on horses by the jailhouse. They have a large wooden box to carry into the woods that'll hold the remains of Misty's body. There are men from all of the surrounding towns. They must have raced in as soon as Sheriff Black got the message out. They're preparing for the horrific journey into the woods by filling canteens, and loading packs and shovels on their horses.

The townsfolk have slowly been making their way back into town, one at a time, to hear the news. Mr. Crawl is hunched over with his head buried in his hands. He's sitting on the a small porch step that leads into the jailhouse. Mrs. Victor is sitting next to him with her arm around his shoulders. She's also wiping the tears from her eyes. Michael wonders how long ago they were informed of the tragedy, and silently grieves Misty's death with them.

Most of the townsfolk are standing around the front door of the store. There are mostly men and young boys with rifles and shovels. Only a few women are in sight. The same lady who wore the green dress, who was in the store earlier that morning, happens to still be there. Michael recalls how kind and efficient she was. Michael and Chloe walk past the law men and the jailhouse, and straight past the angry mob outside the store. They enter the back room of the store where John is sitting at the edge of the bed, waiting for any word from his brother.

"I heard 'um talkin' outside. I know she's dead," John's staring at the floor in front of him with a blank face. "Do they know who done it?" he asks.

"No," Michael answers. "Let's get you home. We can let mom and the women there know what's going on and get your feet up. We'll talk about it all when we get there okay?"

Michael is exhausted, in pain, and ready to lie down himself.

"I'll go outside," Chloe says, "and see if I can find anyone to give us a ride, so you don't have to be on your feet for too long."

Michael squeezes her hand as they part. Chloe looks around for Mr. Smith first, she can't help herself. She's curious to see who he'd be talking to and his demeanor. She also knows he'd be the first person to ask for a ride. She doesn't want him to think she's suspicious of him in anyway. He'd be the first person any of them would approach, given any regular circumstance, so that's exactly her intention.

Mr. Smith isn't anywhere to be seen. Chloe asks around for a few minutes until she runs into Mr. Victor. He jumps at the chance to escape the scene and help out the Hounds brothers. He realizes how intense of a beating they'd each taken earlier that morning. Mrs. Victor had told him all about the shape of the boys when they'd come into the store. Mr. Victor wants to let his wife have more time with Mr. Crawl.

Mr. Victor helps John into the passenger seat of the car. Michael and Chloe climb into the back. During the drive, John sits in silence, letting himself feel the air on his face from the open window. He welcomes the crisp breeze into his lungs. The stinging of his feet and hands are bearable as long as there isn't any pressure on them, but his ribs are a whole different story.

The feeling of an empty hole in his chest is growing bigger and bigger. He pictures Misty's smile and the sparkle in her eye whenever they locked onto his. He'll never see that again, and he never had the chance to let her know what she meant to him. He cannot imagine anyone else ever coming along that could make his heart flutter the way Misty always had. When she does make an appearance, he most certainly won't hesitate to tell her.

There are several children playing ball outside the Hounds house, with their mothers standing close by. Michael breathes a sigh of relief at the normality in it.

"Would you like to come in and have a hot meal?" Michael offers Mr. Victor.

"No son, I'd better get back to the Mrs.," he responds. "Besides, it looks like you have enough mouths to feed as it is. I'll swing by in the morning on my way back into town and see if you need a ride, or help with anything. You know, they're going to have a town meeting around nine. If ya'll wanna' squeeze in, you're welcome to ride along with us."

"Thank you Sir, you and your wife are very kind."

Chloe and John also thank him, before she helps them both hobble into the house. Luckily, one of the women has a large pot of chili on the stove and some cornbread ready to pull from the oven. They enjoy their meal while explaining the terrible events of the day. They tell of their interrogation and of Misty Crawl's body being found in an underground bunker in the woods. The Hounds brothers describe every detail to their mother and the other women in the house, as the children play cards in the other room.

The three of them retreat into the Hounds brothers' cramped

bedroom for the night. The sun drops behind the hills, and the women start to leave two at a time as their husbands show up to escort them home.

"I wonder if they were able to get all of Misty back to town?" John mumbles in the dark. "I hope they can figure out who done it."

They are statements, not questions, and they clearly don't need any kind of response. The three have the weight of the world on their shoulders, and for the time being they can't do a single thing about it. All that's left is sleep. Normally Chloe would sleep on the couch, but tonight's different. Michael wraps himself around her on the top bunk holding her tightly.

"Good night Chloe... my Chloe," he whispers in her ear.

The heat of their bodies pressed so tightly together is almost unbearable for Chloe, but she doesn't care. She'll lay in his arms all night and sleep like a baby.

"I love you Michael." She whispers back.

CHAPTER SEVEN

John slowly opens his eyes. The pain in his hands and feet are even worse than they were the day before. There's an ache in his side and his lip is now scabbed and swollen. He has no intention of leaving home today. Misty has been found and he can't bear to speak to anyone. He'll remain at home with his mother.

She hasn't had the company of either of her sons for an entire day since they were little boys. Under any other circumstances she'd enjoy the help around the house and the company. But, today will be different. Neither of them have much to talk about. Grief, pain, and illness would likely render them awkward and speechless toward each other. It'll be a long day in the Hounds' home for John and his mother.

Michael and Chloe wake to the sound of John sobbing into his pillow. It's awkward, feeling oddly intrusive. To top things off, they're stuck to each other with sweat. The heat of their bodies together is uncomfortable on the stuffy old mattress. Neither of them wants John to know they can hear his sobs, so they lay there, not moving or making a sound. It doesn't last long before Michael can't handle it any longer.

He climbs off the top bunk, leaving Chloe to stretch her legs outside of the smothering blanket. Michael opens the small window to let in the slight morning breeze and much needed fresh air.

"I'll go check on mom, and get you some water, John. Chloe, I'll bet you could borrow some more of my mom's clothes today if you need to."

Michael limps out of the room, wincing from pain once he's out of their sight. Chloe follows close behind him, off the bunk and out of the room. She thinks it best to give John a few minutes to himself.

"Michael, I think I just want to go home and take a bath before that meeting."

It has been a couple days now since she's been home. She's expecting her father and mother to return home from their latest trip any day, and has no clue if they've made it back yet. At the moment, she wants nothing more than to clean up and put on her own clothes. Michael's mom is a size and a half larger than her, and the outfit she's been wearing since the day before is dirty, smells of campfire, hangs off her body, and is now drenched in the mix of her and Michael's sweat.

"Okay, I'll walk with you to your house as soon as I get my mom and brother some breakfast," he says before planting a small peck of a kiss on the tip of her nose.

"Oh no you don't, Michael Hounds."

Mrs. Hounds is standing in the doorway of the kitchen, listening to their every word. Her morning voice is lower and even scratchier than normal, and she's clutching a bloodied cough rag in her frigid fingers.

"I might be sick, but I'm not completely helpless. I can get us our own food and take care of your brother just fine. You go on with Chloe to her house so you have time to make it to that meeting. Its only two hours away and you are walking slowly enough with your limp as it is."

"Mom, I don't think..."

"Don't you back talk me, Michael Hounds. Here, take these and go now before I change my mind and make you stay home and in bed for the day with the rest of us."

There's a demanding tone in her voice that Michael hasn't heard in years. He swallows the two small pain killers that she so eagerly handed over to him. He's well aware that they don't have very many, and that these two measly pills are likely to be the only relief he gets. The few they have left will be for John, and rightfully so, he's in much worse shape.

"Thanks mom. I promise I'll make it to the market as soon as everything dies down."

Michael kisses his mother on the forehead and slips on his shoes.

The two of them walk to Chloe's house slowly, and most of the way in silence. Neither of them is quite sure what to say to each other about the events of the day before. Michael slips Chloe's hand into his and allows a sly grin to take over his face as she blushes and smiles at the touch.

"I can't wait to take a hot bath."

Chloe smirks, knowing that the thought of her naked in the bath would catch Michael's attention. *Two can play at this game*, she thinks.

"Well, maybe I can join you," Michael replies, trying not to giggle.

The color of Chloe's cheeks darkens into a rosy hue, then she smacks him in the chest in reflex. Michael winces and gasps deeply in pain.

"Oh my God. I'm so sorry!"

Chloe places a hand on Michael's chest. He cringes a little at the touch, and reaches up to pull her hand away from the sore spot.

"Maybe we shouldn't kid around until everything calms down and I feel a little better. I guess you're just too violent in nature to take a joke."

Michael holds an arm loosely around the base of his ribs. He glances over at her at out of the corner of his eye. She's glaring at the road ahead of them, her brows pulled downward in the center. He notices the crease in her forehead between them. She has this look every time she gets angry at herself or embarrassed. Michael giggles at the thought.

He really loves Chloe's mad look. It makes her real and genuine in his eyes, not like all the other fake girls his age, who acted like they were someone totally different every time a guy they like comes around. Chloe is undeniably different than any other girl Michael has ever met. He's glad he told her how he feels about her. It's like a weight has been lifted. No more hiding, no more sly glances when she isn't looking.

"What are you laughin' at, gimp?" Chloe shoots him a look of death.

Is he honestly making fun of her for smacking him? she thinks. Chloe hates it every time he gets a kick out of it when she's angry... especially when she's mad enough to stamp around and throw a fit.

"You know, just because I let you kiss me doesn't mean I'm gunna' let you get away with makin' fun of me anytime you want now, Michael Hounds."

"Yes Ma'am,"

Michael pulls his hand up to his forehead, and gives her a salute. His intentions at taking orders aren't very convincing, not with the toothy smile spread across his face. He grabs Chloe's hand and holds it tightly for the rest of the way to the Mead residence. The walkway to the back entrance is long, windy and very well- manicured.

"Wow," Michael says, "it looks like your parents' maid has been busy."

"Yeah she really likes to garden. I think because it gets her out of the house for a while and keeps her busy. My mom got her all the flowers and tools you could dream of before they took off this year. They'll be home anytime, but only for a couple days. Then they're leaving again for Europe until late fall."

Chloe opens the door, exposing the oversized bleach-white entryway to the south wing of her home. There are a couple of cushioned chairs, plastered with floral print sitting against the walls.

Michael sits down, intending to wait for Chloe there. He's never felt comfortable in Chloe's house. It's too big, too clean, and too and impersonal. To Michael it's always seemed more like an empty unwelcomed business building of sorts, rather than a home.

Michael understands why she doesn't like to stay home for long periods of time. Most girls would love the elaborate beauty, but not his Chloe. She's too down to earth for that, too much like himself. Together they appreciate the important things in life, rather than materialistic unnecessities.

"You can at least come and wait in my room, if you want."

She rolls her eyes at uncomfortable fidgeting of Michael's hands and his restless feet. Chloe has never invited Michael to her room. She understands how strange it is for him to be there, and the only time he's ever really come any further into her home than the kitchen was to help her lift something out that she insisted on stealing from her father.

She stares at him for a moment, wondering if everything they had been through together in the last couple of days would change the uncomfortable feeling he had in her home. If they're actually going to be an item, a real item, then he had better get used to it.

Michael returns Chloe's gaze at a loss. He doesn't understand the hold she has over him. The look in her gorgeous blue eyes seems to be peering into his soul. He can't refuse her.

"Ummm, I guess if you want me to," he finally answers.

She reaches for his hand before leading him up the split, winding staircase into the west end of the house. The floors have pink-creamish colored tile and there isn't a smudge of dirt anywhere to be seen. Even if he ever does wind up having as much money as Chloe's father, he'd never waste it on such an impractical mansion.

"Chloe, is that you? hija!" Rosa, the maid, yells from the bottom of the stairs. "You miss you padres. Maybe hour 'go, they leave for next trip already."

Rosa's speaks in a very a broken Spanish. She has a strong accent, one that Michael struggles to understand clearly. Chloe on the other hand, understands Rosa well as she's been the caretaker of herself and the Mead residence for as long as she can remember. Rosa waits at the bottom of the stairs for a few minutes for a response... but hears nothing back from Chloe.

"I tell them you leave wit' Hounds boy days ago. They decide not wait."

Rosa finishes informing the non-responsive Chloe, her instructions for the remainder of the summer, as well as how much money they left her in the safe. Then she walks away, leaving the two of them to their privacy. Rosa and Chloe have a kind and quiet relationship with one another. Rosa knows how Chloe feels about her parents' lack of interest in her whereabouts and clearly doesn't want to push the subject.

Chloe shakes off the stab of rejection from her parents and continues guiding Michael up the stairs. She keeps her chin to her chest so that he can't see her facial expression. A part of Chloe hates her parents for the way they abandon her on a regular basis. The only home she has is with Rosa and the Hounds family. Whenever Chloe is actually home, she stays in her room, only coming out to eat or help Rosa clean and do yard work when she gets bored. She mostly just reads or paints in the solidarity and quiet of her room, her sanctuary.

Michael feels the pain radiate off Chloe. She never really says much about her family or her home life. He has always assumed it was just because she usually so many other things to talk about, or to keep her busy. But now he understands her loneliness, and even the contempt she has for her parents. He also understands why she has absolutely no remorse for stealing from them, or from snooping around her father's office and personal things.

"I'm your family, Chloe."

He says and gives her hand a squeeze. He tries to get a look at her face, but she has it turned too far away from his. She is too proud and stubborn to let him see this side of her. Chloe remains silent until she opens the door to her room. Then she pushes aside the threat of a tear, and finally turns to face him.

"Don't worry about it, Michael, they do it all the time. I'm used to it." Chloe forces a half a smile, but Michael isn't convinced. "Well, here is my room. You can sit and wait for me while I take a bath and get cleaned up. I have my own bathroom through that door so I won't be far, okay?"

"'Kay."

Michael nods and watches her saunter off and disappear to the opposite side of the giant white door she'd pointed at. He mentally measures up the space between the bathroom and her bedroom, guessing that it nearly amounts to the size of his entire hallway. Her bed is way too big for one person to sleep in. It has roses printed all over the comforter. He lies back and lets his body sink into the mattress. *Wow, this bed is awesome,* he thinks. Even if the rest of Chloe's house does make him cringe, he could get used to this bed.

Chloe comes out of the bathroom a while later with her hair still wet and pulled back into a ponytail. She smells like fresh lilac, and her cheeks are still slightly pink from the steam of the bathroom. Michael can't help but stare at her, standing in the doorway looking back at him. Vulnerable and exposed as the woman who's expressed her love for him. She hurries over and lets herself collapse onto the bed next to him.

"You have no idea how much better I feel, she admits.

"I know how much better you smell." Michael giggles and gives her a little nudge to the shoulder before he leans over and plants a kiss on her unsuspecting lips. "Now come on you sexy little thing, we gotta' hurry if we're gunna' make it to the town meeting."

Chloe turns beet red and her eyes widen. Michael has always been able to embarrass her and make her blush, but this new found honesty between the two is putting him on a whole new playing ground. She's stunned by the way he's talking to her and pressing her buttons today, but she likes it. Every time he makes such a remark it sends a surge of energy through her chest. *I could really get used to this,* she thinks. Chloe unsuccessfully tries to wipe the grin off her face as they make their way down the street toward town.

Luckily, they don't make it far before Mr. and Mrs. Victor pull up next to them on the side of the road and ask if they'd like a ride.

"We stopped by your house son, and your mom told us you would be coming from the Mead place. It's a good thing we decided to drive up the lane a ways to make sure. You two never would've made it in time. I have a feeling you'll want to be there after the way Sheriff Black handled things with you and your brother yesterday."

Mr. Victor talks Michael's ears off the whole way to town. The girls merely sit and listen, quietly anticipating what lay ahead.

The pickup is parked to the side of the jailhouse, and they join the fast-growing crowd standing outside the building. The box holding Misty's remains sits ominously on the other side of the building, in the shade of the porch. Chloe can't help but stare at the box, past the small swarm of flies surrounding it. She allows herself to feel guilty for the anger she felt toward Misty when she'd wrongly assumed she was lost. Her heart aches for John and she's glad he isn't there to see the box, just sitting there unattended. Michael stands to the side of Chloe, close enough that their arms press together.

"They should at least put a sheet over it or something," she whispers to him.

Michael nods a simple agreement, and then begins to look around for Steven and Mr. Smith. He changes the subject, refusing to acknowledge such carelessness from the entire town.

"I wonder if Red made it out to the fields to tend to our neighbors' animals this morning. He told me yesterday that he would, since me and John wouldn't be able to. I kinda hope he brought a couple rabbits to my mom for super too."

"Try not to stress about it, if there is anything good about that dumb friend of yours, is that he's dependable. If he told you he'd take care of things, then he did."

Chloe tries her best to reassure him, but she isn't so sure about how convincing it sounds. The truth of the matter is that Chloe isn't so sure of anything today. She feels like anything's possible and nothing would surprise her at this point.

Almost as if right on cue, Steven walks up to them, rubbing the sleep from his eyes.

"Glad ya' made it guys," he says. "I took care of the farmin' this morning. Oh, and be glad you guys left when you did last night. It was the worst and longest night of my life. You wouldn't believe what I had to help all those lawmen pull out of that bunker. I helped 'um take pictures and everything."

Steven looks like he hasn't slept in weeks. His skin is pale, and appears undernourished. With his flesh already being so white and covered in freckles, he now looks almost see thru. For the first time in Chloe's life she feels bad for him.

"I think after this meeting I'm going to go home and rest for a while. I don't know how much longer I can stay awake." Steven mumbles.

"Yeah, that's probably a good idea Red, you look like hell." Michael says.

"Is your dad not going to make it?" Chloe asks.

She tries to make her voice sound casual and disinterested, but she suspects the question came out too eagerly and suspicious. She bites her lip and lets her hands fiddle with the hem of her shirt.

"I don't know. He was locked in his room when I got home last night and he didn't wake up or come out when I left early this morning."

Steven answers Chloe's question with his own wonder and suspicion.

The townsfolk arrive one after another. They even pour in from the neighboring towns. Apparently, the news has spread quickly of Misty's death. There's nearly double the amount of people that there was the morning before, when the bells were rung. Michael assumes it's because most of the wives are now showing up with their husbands, rather than staying behind like many of them did yesterday.

Michael notices many of the women are in their best dresses, with their makeup and hair done up, twisted and braided at the crown of their heads. Chloe must have taken note of the same observations. She leans into his ear and very quietly whispers.

"My God, you'd think this is a beauty pageant, do they not realize there is a dead girl just a few feet away? You'd think they would be trying to chase off a killer instead of attract one."

She is disgusted at the women, standing around chatting as if they were sitting in church on Sunday, waiting for the service to begin. It's as if there isn't a dismembered body a mere couple of yards away.

Michael rolls his eyes, and nods his head in agreement. He too is annoyed, and doesn't understand how a woman's hair could be so important. They stand in silence the rest of the time, just waiting for a lawman to come out and quieten the crowd. Michael and Steven are shoulder to shoulder, with their arms folded and eyes darting through the crowd to take in all the faces.

No one gets too close to the three of them, and the few people from surrounding towns who actually recognize Michael, do so from his fights. Everyone keeps a clear distance, which is perfectly fine to Michael and Steven alike. The swollen eye on Michael's face, and newly formed bruises, just starting to show on his arms, seem to add to the intimidation. Chloe is in her rightful place on the other side of Michael. She feels safe, and comfortable.

Sheriff Black finally steps out of the jailhouse, and onto the porch. He holds his hands high into the air.

"Everyone quiet," he says.

He's sporting giant black rings under his eyes, just like Steven. Also from lack of sleep and nutrition no doubt.

"As you all know, a young woman was brutally murdered the night before last. We found her body mutilated and in an underground bunker yesterday afternoon. Her remains have been looked at piece by piece and we have not been able to find anything that could point us toward who the killer could be. Although, there was one man in the search party that found something that my help our case. Apparently, there is a shack built deep into the woods. It's out past the far west end of town. It is full of stolen items including several weapons, rope and knives. If anyone has any information about this shack please come forward."

Sheriff Black looks around the crowd, trying to avoid locking eyes with Michael. He's still full of shame and guilt for the way he brutally beat Michael and his brother the day before. His body feels like it's aged a few years overnight. The Sheriff waits, eyeing down the crowd in hopes that someone knows something about the strange shed. He truly believes it has to belong to the killer. Who else would hide such items?

The only other explanation would be kids hiding things because they're stolen, but the only kids in town that would hide potential hunting items are the Hounds brothers. He's not about to go there, especially not after the promise he made to Michael about not beating him again.

Chloe steps forward and takes in a breath. She's about to explain the shed she helped to build, and all the items she'd help steal. She intends to explain the innocence of it. But, as she opens her mouth to speak up, Michael grabs her by the hand. He squeezes it hard enough to get her full attention. She looks up at him, shooting daggers from her eyes. He merely shakes his head hoping no one else in the crowd noticed their unspoken moment.

Steven's expression is blank. Chloe understands why Michael doesn't want her to say anything about it being their shed full of tools and hunting items. She disagrees, but understands nonetheless. She looks at his bruised eye, and is completely aware that no one would ever believe their innocence as soon as the Hounds name gets mentioned.

The meeting continues for nearly an hour. Instructions are given for everyone to keep their eyes peeled for anything out of the ordinary. They're told to keep a weapon close at hand and their children indoors until the killer is found and properly dealt with. They discuss the drifters who are still in custody. Sheriff Black reassures the townsfolk that they'll remain in custody until proven innocent or until the true killer is found.

Before the meeting is called to an end, they mention the shed of weapons in the woods one more time, pleading for any information on who it might belong to. Again no one steps forward. The meeting comes to an end, and the more fortunate of the people start back to their cars, horses, and bikes. The majority of the town turns back for their homes on foot.

"I can't wait to get the hell out of this town," Steven says as he hangs his head in defeat and turns to walk home. Michael waits until his friend is out of hearing range before he turns to Chloe.

"Maybe today isn't a good day to go poking around Steven's house. I think maybe we should just lie low today and listen, make sure no one is talking about us with our shed."

Michael knows without a doubt that if anyone finds out the shed belongs to him or his brother they'd be on trial for murder.

"What if they find out it's ours?" Chloe whispers softly.

"We'll just have to figure out what really happened to Misty, before they do."

CHAPTER EIGHT

Steven drags his feet through the front door of his father's house. He takes off his shoes and passes out on the couch right inside the doorway. He is too tired to walk the short distance into his room and doesn't care about the growl in his stomach. The thoughts of Misty's body have been weighing him down. He's still nauseated from everything he witnessed, and that's not to mention the smell. The scent of so much blood and a freshly decaying body isn't something Steven will soon forget.

It was a smell so strong he could taste it. He felt like he'd been breathing in the stench for weeks. No matter how many times he brushed his teeth upon returning home the night before, he still couldn't seem to get the taste out of his mouth. It was overwhelming. He was drenched in her blood from head to toe. Steven can't understand how any human being could do such a thing to another. *What kind of sick and twisted person could cut someone up into pieces?*

When Steven lay in bed the night before he couldn't sleep. All he could think about was how he had to lay out Misty's body like a puzzle, making sure every piece was there. He watched them set her fingers in place, in the order they guessed they would be. He watched them lay her toes next to her feet. Every part of her body was there, in place and accounted for, aside from one toe. He'd helped them search the bunker until it was completely dark and they were all too exhausted to keep going. They'd felt around in the pools of drying sticky blood. They moved around the bones and rotted flesh of the old body that had obviously been there for years. There was no toe to be found.

After having absolutely no sleep all night, and then going out to do all of the Hounds brothers' work this morning, his body finally has just given out. Steven doesn't move from his spot on the couch for hours. He's in a deep and much needed sleep. Upon waking, he opens his eyes briefly to see his father sitting on a chair next to him reading a newspaper as he did every morning before going to work. Steven wonders what time it is. *It has to be in the afternoon, and dad should be at work,* he thinks. He's too tired to give it any more thought, and he drifts back off.

When Steven finally opens his eyes fully, he looks over to see his father still sitting in the same seat.

"Hey, dad. Are you okay?" Steven asks cautiously.

He hasn't spoken to his father since the day before when he and Chloe found the trail that lead to Misty. Steven had pushed the image of his father out of his head as soon as the lawmen showed up in the woods. Helping with Misty's remains took over his mind completely, and until this very moment, he'd forgotten about his father's odd behavior.

"I'm fine son," his voice is short and gruff.

Steven sits up and turns his body at an angle to get a closer look at his father's blank stare. Again, there's an icy glare in his eyes. Steven wonders how long his father has been sitting in this same spot with this thoughtful look on his face.

"What time is it dad?" Steven asks, slowing his words even more.

"Did you know I am going to lose this house?" Mr. Smith responds to Steven speaking, but not with the answer to his question, and with flat unemotional voice. "It's all right there, look." Mr. Smith points at a lone piece of pink paper. It is lying on a miniature coffee table between the two of them. "The store hasn't been able to pay me enough for months. This damn depression is eating us all alive."

Steven picks up the page and reads. The legal document is from the bank and addressed to one Robert Smith. It states that the resident has one month to vacate the property or they will take all the possessions inside as well as the house. The document is dated effective as of three days prior. Steven sits still, frozen in place. This would have been given to his father they day before Misty was taken and murdered in the woods. *Could my dad possibly have anything to do with this?* Steven asks himself.

"I'm going to go see if there's anything I can do to help at the store." Robert states in the same monotone voice. He stands up, and slowly walks out with his head hung and his feet dragging.

Steven stays frozen, unable to take his eyes off the paper. *What would his father do?* He has nowhere to go and no family besides Steven. *Had he snapped under pressure?* Steven shakes the thoughts out of his head. There's no way he can allow himself to think so low of his father. Steven sets the paper back down on the table and retreats into the kitchen for something to eat. It's nearing the evening; Steven had slept the entire day. He wonders if his father had been sitting in the chair next to him the entire time he was sleeping.

Steven contemplates making the few miles walk into town to check on his father and the investigation, but he just can't bring himself to leave the comfort of his father's home. He saunters from room to room, remembering all the good and bad times. He'll likely never see this house again after this summer and he doesn't quite know how to take it all in.

Steven is glad he'll never have to see Mr. Crawl, Sheriff Black or even the Trudge cousins after the next couple weeks when he leaves this town for good. Once he's back home with his mother, there will be no use in coming back. Not now. Not after Misty. He'll never go back into that part of the woods where he spent so many hours the night before.

Steven spends the remainder of the night remembering his past in this town and house. He laughs to himself and is unable to stop a few involuntary tears from roaming the length of his face, as the memories surface. Then he sits on the porch in solitude to watch the sun go down. He waits up for a few hours, hoping to speak to his father before crashing into bed for the night, but his father never shows up.

Steven wakes up the next morning, bright and early to a knock on the door. He swings it open to see Chloe and Michael standing hand in hand.

"Well, I can't say I'm surprised," Steven proclaims rolling his eyes at the love birds standing in front of him. "Come on in guys, have you had breakfast?" Steven asks, trying without success to sound upbeat and hospitable.

"Yeah, Rosa made us breakfast."

Michael is unable to hide the smirk that came along with the remark.

Steven assumes, correctly, that meant Michael had spent the night at Chloe's house. This is yet another unwelcome surprise for Steven. Everything he knows about this place is changing, and fast.

"How did you guys get here so early? You must have left before the sun even came up."

"We drove," says Michael.

"What do you mean, you drove?" Steven is confused, but he doesn't have the energy, or the ambition to really care much about the answer.

"My dad gave me a car a few months ago." Chloe confesses, and drops her chin to her chest. "I put the keys back on the table when he handed them to me and told him I didn't want it. I forgot all about it until this morning when Rosa reminded me. She didn't want Michael to have to walk in pain."

"How the hell could you forget you had a car... just given to you?" Steven asks, equally in shock as he is irritated.

"My father's always buying me stupid pointless things."

"I wouldn't call a car stupid, or pointless."

"That's exactly what I said," Michael jumps in.

Chloe breathes in with a sigh, and then lets it deflate, along with her dignity.

"I don't know," she confesses, "I guess I just feel like they are buying *me*."

Chloe looks down, her eyes fixated on the laces of her shoes. She's wholly embarrassed to be telling her friend about how spoiled she is. Especially since they have to scrimp and save just to eat. She's been turning down her father's gifts since she was little. Chloe doesn't want to be anything like her parents and is determined to make her own way in life. She doesn't even like to be in this stupid car, and insisted first thing this morning, that Michael drive. Anything to help her feel like she isn't accepting the way her parents buy her love.

This is the first summer that Chloe can remember actually getting along with Steven. A part of her has even enjoyed his company. The last thing Chloe wants to do is push away his friendship by bragging and rubbing it in that she comes from money.

Steven shrugs, "well, I guess if you're gunna' take something they give you, it might as well be a car."

A part of Steven is still too shaken up about his father and their house to care much about Chloe's car, and a part of him doesn't dare be rude or show any jealousy because he doesn't want to set off Michael. Steven has always drawn a line across the things he will or won't say to Chloe.

They need a car now more than ever, so if that means Chloe has to swallow her pride and accept it, then so be it. As much as she hates to admit it, she's now actually grateful for the gift. Not only do they need the time saver, but with Michael being hurt, and a killer on the loose, they need the security and safety of it.

They have to find Misty's killer before they wind up being accused themselves, *again*, because of their shed in the woods. Not only that, but they aren't able to use anything out of the shed in the process. There's no way they can risk being seen getting in and out of it. There is sure to be lawman, standing post watching, just in case someone shows up to claim their goods.

"Is your dad home?" Michael asks Steven.

"No, I haven't seen him since yesterday. He said he was going to check on the store last night, but then he still hasn't come back home." Steven runs a hand through his messy hair. "He's been acting really strange, and then he told me yesterday that he's losing the house to the bank."

"Wow, I am so sorry Red," Michael says.

"Yeah I think I'm going to go look for him. Maybe he stayed at the store or something. Do you guys mind staying here in case he comes back?" Steven asks. "Just for a little while, anyway?"

"Sure." Chloe answers quickly, and perhaps a little too anxiously.

Again, she looks at her feet, not wanting Steven to notice her excitement. She has been scheming and plotting possible ways to get both Steven and his father out of their house at the same time. And, now the opportunity has presented itself without even any effort on her or Michael's part. Chloe holds her breath, hoping he doesn't notice her nerves.

She peeks over at him out of the corner of her eye. Steven shows no sign of suspicion. He puts on his hat and walks out the door. Neither Chloe nor Michael can recall any time they've seen him look so down. Steven's posture is slumped at the shoulders, and the bags under his eyes are dark and saggy. Unhealthy is the only word that comes to Chloe's mind to describe the way Steven looks this morning.

"Hey, Red," Michael calls Steven's attention back before he has a chance to shut the door behind him, "take the car."

Michael tosses the keys through the open door, and watches his friend grab them from the air.

"Thanks man," he mumbles before dumping his hands in his pockets and walking away with the door left wide open.

Chloe and Michael follow him outside and take a seat on the porch. They watch the tail end of Chloe's car disappear down the lane. They wait until he's completely out of sight before they run back into the house, racing down the stairs into the creepy basement.

"Wait," says Michael. "Are you sure we should be doing this?"

"Are you kidding me, Michael Hounds? This isn't the first time we've broke into this room, remember?" Chloe points out. "Plus, there's a lot at stake here."

"Yeah, but this time Red isn't with us. It just feels, I don't know... wrong!" Michael is nervous and worried. He drums his fingertips on his thigh.

"I don't think we have a choice."

Chloe holds her gaze on Michael, compassion showing from the downward pull of the corners of her eyes. She too is scared, shaking even, but some things just have to be done.

"Okay, but we gotta hurry. We can't get caught down here Chloe, we just can't."

Chloe opens the lock in record time. She takes a deep breath and concentrates on her nervous hands. She steadies them and focuses. She listens closely for the clicking noises coming from the handle of the door as the lock comes undone. The door creaks open and there they stand.

They're in the same place, looking at the same shelves in the small room they had been a few weeks before. Only this time, John and Steven are missing and the shelves are completely empty. All that's remaining is the box of newspapers that they had left sitting on the floor.

"See, I knew we didn't miss anything when we took all the stuff Chloe, now let's just get out of here."

Michael, grabs her arm and starts pulling her toward the doorway. Of course, Chloe doesn't budge.

"No wait."

Chloe searches the empty shelves from top to bottom.

"All the dust is gone, Michael. He had to have come in here and cleaned after we took all the stuff. Why wouldn't he mention to Steven that they were robbed unless he was hiding something?"

"Good point" Michael agrees. He too looks blankly at the shelves in wonder, then mumbles to himself. "Something doesn't make sense about this whole thing."

Something doesn't make sense about Robert Smith, Chloe thinks.

"I'm gunna' go look down the road, in case Steven or his dad are coming back." Michael says, just before running back up the steps two at a time.

Chloe runs a finger across an empty shelf, trying to make sense of this strange locked away room in Mr. Smith's basement. "I just don't get it," she whispers to herself.

Chloe picks up the top newspaper in the box and begins to read. The words all but jump off the pages at her. It's all starting to come together.

"Oh my God," she whispers.

Michael comes bounding back down the steps.

"The coast is clear. Now, let's get out of here, please."

"Hold on." Her face is still buried in the paper.

"I'm serious, Chloe. Let go."

"Look at this." She tells him, and holds one of the articles up to his face. "Each of these papers have an article circled about a murder. Look at the dates."

Chloe points at the date at the top of the newspaper Michael is now ripping from her hands, it reads 1921. This was a couple years before they were born. Chloe digs through looking at the dates on each paper. They all range in dates, covering an eight-year span. The most recent one she can find is dated 1927. Chloe reads the full article on this paper.

"Michael, this one is about the girl that was stabbed when the clinic was blown up, do you remember that? All these murders took place within a day's drive from here."

They sit in the dingy basement, going through each paper as quickly as possible, trying to piece any clues together. Once in a while, one or the other would run up the steps to check the lane.

"We've been down here reading for too long Chloe. We have to get out of here before Steven or his dad show back up."

"You're right. We have to tell Steven that his dad has all of these papers. Do you think he has something to do with it?" She asks while tucking them all neatly back into the box.

"I don't know. Let's just go."

Just as they take the last step at the top of the stairs, they hear the sound of tires pulling into the driveway. They rush to the couch to make themselves look as innocent as possible. Steven walks through the door first, with Mr. Smith following a close step behind. Chloe's heart is pounding and her hands shake on her lap. Robert Smith is drunk as a skunk and stumbling over his feet.

"Come on Dad, let me help you to your room."

Steven struggles to put an arm under his father's armpit, and help steady him on his feet.

"Nonsense!" Mr. Smith shouts in Steven's face and tosses his son's hand aside. "I don't want to go to bed, it's the morning time. I want to talk to your nosy thieving friends". He blurts, and wags an angry finger in their direction.

The drunken Robert Smith shoves his son against the wall before turning to face Chloe and Michael on the couch. Chloe gasps and pulls her legs to her chest. Michael stands up, ready to face Steven's father toe to toe if necessary.

"Sir, we're not thieves" Michael lies. "Come on Chloe, I think our welcome here has worn out."

Michael pulls Chloe off the couch, and pushes her behind his back. Broken ribs or not, he's prepared to throw a fist or two if needs be.

"Red, are you coming with us or not?" Michael looks at Steven, sternly pulling his brows together.

He wills Steven to pick up on the look, not wanting to leave his best friend behind. He needs to know what the newspapers say in the basement. He needs to get away from Robert Smith, but how can they make him without physically pulling him away?

"Hellll no, he'sss not goin'!" Shouts Mr. Smith with a slur.

He raises his hand to point another angry finger in Michael's face, but is unable to finish his sentence. He passes out face first onto the floor, stiff as a board.

"I'd better stay and take care of him." Steven says, his words dripping in defeat. "He's too drunk to do anything to me anyway, I'll be fine."

"But Steven you can't stay here," Chloe starts to say in a panic. Michael jumps in and interrupts her before she has a chance to reveal anything about what they'd just found.

"It's okay, Chloe. Let's go and let Steven take care of his dad. I'm sure he'll be passed out for a while and when he wakes up, he'll be more reasonable." He shoots Chloe a look that makes her shut her mouth instantly. "You're sure this is what you want to do?" he asks Steven one last time before they walk out the door.

"Yeah, I'll be fine guys. I'll meet up with you later."

"M'kay, we won't be far. We were able to run out to the trading market with Mr. Victor yesterday, and now all the old farmers are taking care of their own land and animals until all of this mess is figured out, so you'll be able to find us without trouble. We have nowhere to go."

Michael nods his head at the basement door, and points with his eyes in its direction the whole time he talks to Steven. He makes it obvious that they'd found something without saying a word out loud. He doesn't dare give anything away, not right next to Mr. Smith. Passed out or not, he doesn't want to risk being heard. Steven's lips form a hard line, full of speculation. He nods an understanding before saying anything back to his friend.

"Okay, I better get him to bed. I'll meet up with you later."

Steven hooks a thumb toward the basement, and the two nod and mouth an eager, *yes*. Chloe lets out a breath of relief when he catches onto their unspoken gestures. She feels a little bit better about leaving Steven alone with his dad. Chloe can't decide what to think about the newspapers, and has put Mr. Smith at the top of her own personal suspect list. *Steven can read the articles for himself while his dad's sleeping,* she thinks, *at least then he'll know something strange is up with the man.*

Michael and Chloe slowly inch away from the Smith home. Chloe stares out the back window at Steven with a lone tear streaking down her face. She's overwhelmed, and an ominous feeling of finality is lumping in the pit of her belly.

Steven mozies out to the porch with his hands in his pockets, and the look of a lost puppy on his face. He doesn't want to go back in the house and deal with his father. Mr. Smith had stayed up all night and drunk himself into a frenzy. He stayed in the back room of the store, downing bottle after bottle of cheap booze until Steven showed up and drove him home.

As soon as his friends are out of sight, Steven goes back inside. He takes a good long look at his father on the floor of their living room. Steven is grateful that his dad is drunk to the point of passing out, rather than being coherent and angry. He doesn't have the energy to fight with him. He's also disturbed and scared at his father's behavior over the last few days.

Steven grabs his father by the arms and drags him down the hall and into his room. He doesn't bother to take off his father's shoes or to lift him onto his bed. *I'll just let him sleep it off on the floor,* he thinks. Steven then stops at the top of the basement stairs. He takes a deep breath, preparing himself before he takes the first step into the unknown.

CHAPTER NINE

C hloe cries the whole way down the road until they pull into town. She's trying to convince herself that they did the right thing by snooping, and by leaving Steven's basement door unlocked for him to follow suit. Michael drives in silence, trying to take in all the new information.

"I think we should stop at the store and see if anyone has heard anything else out about our shed." He says.

Chloe nods an agreement before he takes the turn down the lonely center street of their small town. There are men standing on the corner of almost every building holding their rifles and pistols. They stare at Michael and Chloe as they make their way down the road. Some with faces as hard as stone, and some spit on the ground at their feet.

"I don't like the way they're looking at you," Chloe says.

"It's okay. I'm sure they look at everyone driving down the road this same way. It doesn't mean anything, Chloe. Plus, they've never seen this car before, I don't think they like that I'm driving a new car."

Michael looks ahead, making a conscious effort to avoid eye contact with any of the men trying to stare him down. *Just stay focused,* he thinks to himself. Michael can't appear to have any reason to stay away from town. He knows that he has to be the same as everyone else around, and not let on that the shed of weapons belongs to him.

From the moment he pulled out of the Mead driveway that morning, Michael had a gut feeling that his life would again change for the worse. He's fully aware that the local farmers and townsmen would treat him differently. As of today, everyone would know that he is no longer just a friend of that loud mouth little Mead girl. He now has the richest girlfriend within a five county range.

Everyone would be angry. They're all starving, and one at a time becoming sick and homeless. They're losing small children to disease and struggling for each meal. Michael is well aware that the surrounding farmers would no longer allow him, or his brother, to help them out around their farms for any kind of pay. The only reason the Hounds boys have been able to find work up until this point, is because the level of respect the town has for their mother.

Michael understands wholeheartedly that being with Chloe as a couple, puts him in a new category. Not only would he be loathed or treated differently by everyone he knows around town, but he'd also soon suffer the repercussion from her family. Michael understands the fact that Chloe will never accept help or handouts from her parents, and eventually he'll would have to support and take care of her a hundred percent. *She's worth it,* he thinks.

Chloe also knows all of these facts to be true, and they are yet to actually discuss it. Everyone is staring and she too understands the unspoken reasoning. It's all because of her, and her family's money. She knew that people would eventually treat him differently, but now? *Amidst everything that's happened this week, how could everyone be so cold over money?* She doesn't understand, and how could she? Chloe has never lost loved ones to hunger, or even gone hungry herself.

The thought of Michael and John not having work due to her,

makes her stomach churn. Chloe hadn't given that particular angle any thought until now, and the reality of it hits her like a plague. Eventually she'll have to accept money from her parents. Circumstance will call for it, just like it did with the car. Chloe dreads the quickly approaching day with all of her being. She opens her mouth to talk about it, but her lips snap shut just as fast. *Not now,* she can't find the words.

She looks around at all the men and women, memorizing the details of their faces. At least she does have an option to fall back on. Her parents may not have been a pillar of love, but they *are* there, and so is their money. Chloe feels a stab to her chest as she truly realizes, clear to her core, that these people have no option to fall back on. *And what makes Michael and I worse in their eyes,* she wonders, *accepting handouts or actually turning something away that they'd kill for the opportunity to have?* It's lose all around. Who would think love could be such a double-edged sword?

Chloe thinks about Misty, and the fact that she never had a chance either. She came from a starving family in a poor household just like everyone else around. A part of Chloe feels guilty that she's always taken her 'family money' for granted. She feels bad for turning her back to the fortune when anyone else around would be happy to have even a quarter of the privilege she's been handed. Chloe is suddenly unable to look into their faces. Her heart is wrenched for each of them, and she's embarrassed to be driving around in this car that she neither earned, nor deserved.

They park next to Mr. Smith's car, that's been left by the store. Michael holds his head high, and grabs Chloe's hand to lead her into the store.

"Never mind all the looks Chloe, I love you and I always have," he tells her. "You'll never be anything like your parents!"

He wipes a tear from her soft cheek, and plants a gentle kiss where it had lingered. Michael opens the door, takes a long look into her eyes, understanding the quiet pain behind them. He then turns and enters the store. He doesn't push her for a conversation about it, and never will, but he can see behind her shield. He knows exactly what is eating at her.

Chloe appreciates Michael's effort to make her feel better, though she's never felt so shallow and spoiled in all her life. Chloe just can't understand what her parents enjoy so much about having more money, and being more fortunate than others. She doesn't understand what they could possibly love about parading around like they are better than everyone else.

Mrs. Burns, the store owner's wife, looks up from behind the counter as they walk in.

"Oh, hello Michael, you look much better than you did the other day. I take it you have gotten some rest?"

She's a kind woman. She speaks in a soft, welcoming voice and seems genuinely concerned. An old man walks out as they walk in. He glares at Michael, sizing him up from top to bottom on his way out. Then he glances over at Chloe and rolls his eyes, mumbling under his breath.

"What the hell are you looking at?" Chloe snaps at him, on his way out. She can't help herself. She feels bad enough, having to accept her parents hand out, she doesn't need to take any crap from the townsfolk about it too.

"Oh, never mind him dear," Mrs. Burns smiles at Chloe. "I'm glad you finally decided to admit to yourselves that you belong together. I've been watching you two since you were tots. Sure do make a cute couple."

"Thanks ma'am," Chloe grins back at the old lady.

"Have you heard anything new from any of the lawmen?" Michael cuts to the chase with Mrs. Burns. Despite her kindness, has no need or desire to sit around and small talk.

"Just that Sheriff Black finally up and fired Deputy Evan. Apparently he put in for a replacement months ago and hasn't heard anything back. The Deputy got caught by one of the other lawmen poking around that poor girl's remains last night." Mrs. Burns shakes her head in disgust. "Robert came in just as I was closing up shop. He was just starting in on a bottle of whiskey. Apparently, he was watching Deputy Evan get into that God-awful box sitting outside the jailhouse with Misty's body in it. Robert saw the whole thing. He asked me if he could stay here for the night and keep an eye on the lawmen. Of course, I let him."

Mrs. Burns talks and talks about how she isn't surprised at the Deputy, and about how drunk Mr. Smith was when she came back in this morning. No one really understands why they were yet to bury Misty's body. No-one but Sheriff Black, who thus far has refused to give an explanation on his determination to keep her top side. The box has been left in the sun to rot.

One thing about Mrs. Burns is that she isn't a woman of little words. She would tell anyone anything they ask. Mrs. Burns would talk to any one person for hours if they let her. She also pays close attention to details. Michael and Chloe listen to her every word, waiting for her to mention or say anything more about their shed in the woods, but she never brings it up. Relieved for the update and the fact that there still aren't any fingers pointed in their direction, Chloe and Michael say their goodbyes to Mrs. Burns.

"Oh, I almost forgot." Chloe runs back into the store and hands Mrs. Burns two dollars. "Will you please use this money the next time Mr. and Mrs. Victor fill up their car with gas?" Chloe asks.

"I sure will honey, are you sure you want to pay this much? That is way more than what they've used the little distance they drove you and those Hounds boys around. You know this is enough to completely fill up their tank." Mrs. Burns hesitates, but takes the money from Chloe nonetheless.

"I'm sure, ma'am. You and the Victor family have treated us better than anyone else in this damned ol' town. You're the only ones who even bothered askin' how John is feelin' too. Oh, and if you don't mind keeping it between us too, ma'am? I mean, I know they'll be able to guess where it's comin' from, but I don't want anyone else to know."

Mrs. Burns gives Chloe a pointed look and nods her understanding. She knows exactly why Chloe doesn't want any credit for her generosity. The old woman simply slips the dollar bills into her skirt pocket.

"I'll make sure to spend a few cents of it for some of that pink material over there, too. I know Mrs. Victor has wanted to make herself a dress with it for quite some time."

Mrs. Burns follows her statement with a wink.

"Thanks again, ma'am," Chloe says, as she strolls back out the door.

She climbs into the passenger seat of the car, and Michael starts the engine. The men and women seemed to have gotten over their initial reaction to Michael and Chloe pulling into the town in a new car. He hopes they've accepted the situation for what it is. Besides, they have more important things to deal with today than the rich teenage girl of the town, and her new boyfriend.

"I'm really worried about Steven." Chloe says. "I just can't decide what to make of all those newspaper articles. Do you really think Mr. Smith is capable of murder?"

"It doesn't look very good, Chloe. We're gunna' need more than just a couple newspaper articles to prove anything though."

"Maybe after Steven reads um' all, he'll come find us, and we can make some sense of it all." Chloe digs a little bit of logic. "I sure am glad Deputy Evan is fired! That smelly ol' fat ass had it comin'."

"Yeah me too! I wonder what he was doin' lookin' at Misty's body parts like that. They otta' just bury her already. I don't understand why they think they need to keep it in that nasty ol' box." Michael shakes his head in disgust. "I could smell it all the way over by the store."

"I didn't want to say anything in front of Mrs. Burns," Chloe says, "but, I overheard a couple of farmers at that meeting yesterday say they were using it as bait to see if the killer came to it. He said it was a classic trick and it worked every time."

Chloe recalls straining to hear them talk over all the other chatty women they were standing next to. *Stupid women*, Chloe thinks.

"I wonder what that sick Deputy Evan wanted with it," she continues. "He's such an evil bag a shit. He was probably wondering what her parts looked like after being dead for a couple days." Chloe has a chill run through her body as she says it out loud.

"Probably," Michael agrees, nodding his head. He leans to the side, and with one hand on the wheel, he places the other on Chloe's knee. "So, if they are actually using her body as bait, that gives us one more reason to suspect Steven's dad. I mean, why else would he want to stay at the store and keep an eye on things."

"You're right, Michael ... shit! It makes sense." She reaches down and squeezes his hand. "I think if we don't see or hear from Steven, we need to go check up on him."

The two pull up to the Hounds' home. They sit in the car for a few minutes in silence, thinking. Michael glances over at her, studying the concerned look planted on her face. *God she is beautiful,* he thinks. Chloe is heartbroken for Misty's family and can't get over the fact that the lawmen are just letting her body rot in the summer heat, right in the middle of town. The tactic makes sense, but the morality is all wrong. Chloe can't wrap her mind around the evil of this place. She wishes she could run away until it's all over.

CHAPTER TEN

Steven read each article twice over. He can't believe what he's seeing. What reason could there possibly be for his father to have such a fortress locked away in his home? Steven imagines the room before they'd taken everything out of it. He pictures the crossbows, all the arrows, the knives, and even the rope. He can't help but to imagine that same rope, being used to tie up any of these women he read about.

Steven wonders if the same knives he's used to skin rabbits for the past few weeks were ever used to slice a throat or cut off an arm. The thought makes Steven sick to his stomach. He read on about the stabbings and dismembering of girls' bodies. He can't help but remember in detail, every part of Misty's body that he'd helped to carry up the ladder and out of that awful hole in the ground. There are two articles that read the women were never found.

The old bones left behind in that bunker, could easily belong to either of those women. There was only one skull, so they assumed there is only the remains of one woman. But it seemed to Steven like there were way too many ribs to only belong to one person. He wishes now that they would have counted them. Steven has lost track of time, as he's unable to put the newspapers down. He is sitting there in the basement reading them over and over, he can't peel himself away.

The burning look in his father's eyes is drumming in the back of his mind as he reads, as well as his mother's words of warning, *'he's a good man, Steven, and a good father. Just don't cross him.'* Steven takes a few deep breaths and sets the papers down. Steven stares into space for only God knows how long. He feels lost and unsafe in his own home. His mind is playing tricks on him, only the thoughts are backed by distorted reality.

Suddenly, out of nowhere, Mr. Smith's voice sounds from behind Steven's back at the middle of the stairway.

"Son, where is the rest of it?"

Goosebumps rise on his arms. Steven doesn't know whether to run or yell. Maybe he should fight his now sober and well rested father. Rather than doing any of these things, Steven freezes in place. He's unable to breathe or move. Every muscle in his body seems to be paralyzed with fear. Steven listens to the sound of his father's breathing, followed by his steps growing closer and closer to the bottom of the stairs. One step at a time, each stair he takes slower than the last. It feels like his father's creeping up to him, as if stalking his next prey.

"Well, answer me boy. Where are the rest of my things?" Steven's father repeats the question, a little louder and more demanding.

"I. I. I. don't know sir," Steven stammers.

Robert Smith, now standing directly over his son, looks down the back of his shaking body. Steven is sitting cross legged on the floor. A small puddle of liquid slowly forms underneath him. He doesn't even notice that he's peeing all over himself. He's never been so afraid in his life. Steven had witnessed firsthand the work of a brutal killer. Now, he's sitting at his father's feet surrounded by proof that he could very easily be the man capable of doing such unspeakable things to Misty Crawl.

This is it, this is the end of my life, Steven thinks, *this'll be my last breath.* His body falls numb, tingly with anticipation. He closes his eyes and tries to picture his mother in what he assumes to be his last moments. Sitting in the shadow of his very tall father, Steven can feel the heat coming from his body.

"Well, I guess pissing yourself is probably worse punishment than what I would have given ya." Mr. Smith begins to snicker, and it soon grows into a full-on laugh at his teenage son sitting in a puddle at his feet. "Put all those papers back in the box, son. Bring it all upstairs. It looks like we both have some explaining to do."

Mr. Smith turns around with his arm over his mouth, trying to muffle his humor as he leaves Steven to catch his breath.

"What the hell just happened?" Steven says in a quiet voice to himself.

There he sits in a puddle of his own urine. His father was right. This could possibly be the most embarrassing moment of Steven's life. Steven swears if he's ever in this situation again he'd fight rather than freeze up and pee himself like a baby.

Once his heart rate slows down a bit, Steven scoops up the papers, drops them in the old box and carries them up the steps. He drops the box on the table in front of his waiting, and still chuckling father.

"You sure can lighten the mood, boy." Mr. Smith teases. "This could be the most emotional week that both of us have ever had, yet here I am laughing, and there you are covered in pee."

Steven storms off to his room to clean up and change his clothes. He can't recall the last time he heard his father laughing. On several occasions, he's tried to tease and joke around with his dad. Robert Smith is usually a kind and sociable man, but he rarely has the plea-sure of downright laughable humor. Steven is grateful for the change of mood in his father. Even if he has to completely humiliate himself in the process, it's taken away some of the weight of spec-ulation.

Steven knows his father wouldn't tell a soul about their little encounter, the pee will likely stay between the two of them. He's also curious to hear his father's reasoning for having all the weapons and news articles. Fresh undies and jeans are quickly put on before Steven heads back for the kitchen to join his dad.

Robert moved the kitchen table outside, and is laying each news-paper on the floor. Steven stands in the doorway, watching his father organize each paper by date. He stops when he is nearing the end, and holds up the second to last paper in the box. Robert runs his hand over the picture that is circled in black and white ink. He stares at it with a lost and mournful look in his eyes.

"Who is that, dad?" Steven asks

"This was my sister, Steven, your aunt."

Steven's father hands him the paper and tells him to read. Ruth Ann Gene Smith was her name. She was taken from her home in the middle of the night. She was only 20 years of age. Steven reads her name over and over, and studies her face. He can see the similarities between this old picture and his now aged father.

They had the same slope in their noses, and their smile had the same uneven lift on one side. Steven had read the article more than once while he sat in the basement. He now wondered how he hadn't put together their last name and the ways she looked so much like his father.

"The other bones in that hole could very well belong to her, Steven." Robert exclaims.

Mr. Smith explains to Steven how she was the first to be taken. He tells his son about how he became obsessed with finding whoever took her. He collected newspapers from the entire state, watching for any other girls who had gone missing or were murdered. He would circle each article he came across and read it every day looking for similarities. He spoke about his wife, Steven's mother, and how she became angry at him. She couldn't handle the obsession and they'd fight about it regularly.

"I didn't blame her when she left, son, but I didn't try to stop her either." He says, and takes a long drink of iced water in effort to rehy-drate his hungover body. "The more we'd fight, the more I took all of the frustration of my sister's disappearance out on her. It only took one time smacking her across the face, and she was gone. I bloodied her lip and let her walk away."

Honesty oozes from Mr. Smith, and the solidarity in his voice is thick. Steven looks at his father with compassion. He feels sorry for his dad, and a strong sense of grief for the aunt he's never heard of.

Steven's father pauses for a few moments in thought. It seems to Steven like he may actually be remembering good times for a brief moment, and then a dark shadow moves over his face. Steven watches as his father's demeanor changes from what could have been, to what is now. An icy glare takes over Robert Smith as he continues.

"It wasn't until I seen Deputy Evan sneaking in to see that Crawl girl's body that I put it all together." He says in a deep and disturbing voice.

Robert explains how Deputy Evan had lived here years ago when all these murders took place. He tells Steven about how Evan was not a man of the law at the time. Evan had been a jobless bum. No one ever understood where he got money to live, and suspected him to be a thief on several occasions. Evan didn't have any friends, and was a filthy man back then, the same as he is now. It wasn't until he had lived in Texas about five years back that he became a man of the law.

He has a knack for sketching. Stinky Deputy Evan could sketch the face of anyone explained to him in enough detail and it came in handy in his new found profession. As soon as Sheriff Black sent out a telegram to several states that he was looking for a new Deputy that Evan moved back. Deputy Evan couldn't wait to get back to this town. It was his favorite place that he'd lived in. One good thing about Robert Smith working at the only store around, is that he knew every detail about everyone in town.

According to Mr. Smith, Deputy Evan moved away shortly after the Clinic was burned to the ground. Everyone knew that whoever had harmed the girl inside the clinic at the time of the incident had to be the arsonist as well.

"Sheriff Black had just barely been sworn in as Sheriff at the time. He'd only investigated one murder before hers, and he was dumber then than he is now." Robert continues. "They never found any leads on the man who had tortured the girl, and they never found out who threw the dynamite into the Clinic."

Steven's father hands him the newspaper containing the story of the girl who had been stabbed and tortured nearly to death. The girl had somehow escaped from her kidnapper and passed out from loss of blood in front of the clinic. The dynamite had exploded and killed her before she could actually talk to anyone, tell them her story, or give them any information about her attacker. For some reason the murders and kidnappings stopped after her.

"You had just turned five years old at the time, Steven," Mr. Smith explains. "Within a couple years after that, I locked away the newspapers along with the weapons and decided to focus on being a father. I had already lost my wife and my only sister. I wasn't about to lose my son too."

Mr. Smith hangs his head in shame and embarrassment as he speaks. Then he looks up and locks eyes again with Steven.

"Then all of the sudden, years later out of nowhere, the Crawl girl disappeared. I went straight to the basement as soon as I had a chance to go through the papers so I could try to put things together, and everything else in the room was missing." He holds his gaze with Steven. "Well, where is it?"

"I'm so sorry dad, please don't be mad," Steven pleads before he explains.

"There's no time to be mad at each other, son. There are more important things for us to deal with."

"I don't understand, why did you have all of that stuff anyways?"

Steven asks, before confessing to what they had done with his father's things. He understands now the papers, but Steven still can't place what his father could possibly want with all that other stuff. It is a major hole in Robert Smith's story.

"I was going to find the man who took my sister, and do every-thing to him that he had done to each of these girls." Robert points at all the papers scattered across their kitchen floor. Again, his voice escapes him with an eerie emotionless look on his face, and a burning hate in his eyes. "I wanted him to suffer the same way his victims had.... I still do.... Now where is it all Steven?"

He is growing impatient with his sons stalling. There is a lot to do, he feels as if all the emotions he'd experienced years before are coming back. Scratching their way to the surface. Robert knows the killer has to be Deputy Evan, *it has to be*. He moved away when the killings stopped, and now that he is back, girls are once again being murdered. It's as simple as that.

Steven's voice is timid, like a small child.

"We took it all, and put it in a shed in the woods."

His father promised not to be angry, but previous experience tells Steven something completely different. He can see the anger filling up in his father as he confesses everything. He tells his dad about how Chloe picked the lock, and about how they'd built the shed a couple of summers ago. They've been storing everything they've stolen in it. Steven lets go of everything that's been on his chest the last few days. Everything about the Lawmen finding the shed and about how they needed to find the real killer before the finger gets pointed to the Hounds brothers and to him.

"We have to go to Deputy Evans house, son."

Robert pulls himself to his full six-foot five height, and guzzles another long drink of his water. The emptied glass is set back on the table with a *clank*. He contemplates how to go about getting there without being noticed, even for just a moment, he then looks at the scared teenage boy standing next to him.

"I know you're scared, boy... but you can't freeze up like you did earlier. I thought it was funny at the time, but now it just scares the hell out of me. You need to be strong. You're just as deep into this as me now, and I'm not going to be having my boy accused of murder."

"Yes, sir."

"Get your shoes on, let's go now. If Sheriff Black really fired Evan this morning then there'll be nothing to hold him back or stop him from taking anyone else before he skips town."

Certainty shines through Robert's voice. If he's ever going to have a chance to avenge his sister's death, that chance is now. Nothing can keep him from the opportunity.

They ready themselves quickly. In only a few short moments their shoes are on and their pistols are tucked into holsters on their belts. Each with a steady hand, and a skinning knife in their pockets. They grab a slice of bread to eat on their way out the door, not knowing when they'll have time for a full meal.

"Too bad you had to be driving that spoiled little girl's car this morning, or you would've been able to take mine home. We wouldn't have to be on foot right now, huh?"

Robert acts like its Steven's fault he was falling over, passed out drunk that morning. It's selfish and careless, he knows that, but he is not capable of taking responsibility for his mistakes.

Steven doesn't say a word to his father about the episode at the store that morning. He had to practically carry his ranting and raving father out of the public eye. He also doesn't mention the way his father had treated his friends during the drunken rage, before he fell over face first. Steven shuts his mouth, not wanting to distract his father or give him any ammunition to turn on him, especially after the last half an hour of honesty between the two of them. Mr. Smith isn't in his right mind, and who knows, he could snap at any time. Steven will have to walk on eggshells, and he hopes it would not be for long.

They make their way to town in record time on foot. Robert Smith is an angry and determined man. There'd be no stopping him today. He finally has the chance to deal with the man who took his sister years before, to avenge her death. Robert has built himself up for this moment for years. Countless nights have been spent imagining the torture he'd inflict and what he'd say to him as he did it. Robert has dreamt of the day he could inflict as much pain as possible, for as long as possible, without actually killing him. He'd make sure that his sister's killer would relive every moment of pain he'd handed out to all those women.

"This way," Robert says, taking a sharp turn into the trees just before reaching town. "Evan's house is at the end of that long skinny trail behind the jailhouse. He walks to work every day, there are no roads that go in or out. If we go this way, we can probably get there without being seen. We'll have to be quiet though, I'm sure all of the outside lawmen have camps close by."

Mr. Smith speaks quietly and steadily. He's on the hunt.

Steven and his father sneak through the trees on the outskirts of town. It won't look good if they're caught sneaking around. He quiets and quickens his every steps. He also makes a conscious effort to steady his breath, and repeats in his head over and over. *Don't freeze Steven, this is it, don't freeze.* His hands are now shaking and his legs feel heavy.

They get a few feet away from the Deputy's house and wait. Steven follows his dad's lead in silence. He's determined to help his dad do whatever needed to catch his aunt's and Misty's killer. They watch the windows for movement for several minutes and can't see a thing. Robert draws his gun, and tells Steven to wait where he is.

"If you hear shots, boy, be really quiet and look in every window before you enter the house. Listen closely and be prepared for anything."

He left his son behind, with nothing but his words of advice, and walks up to the back door... ready to shoot if needed.

Steven waits, watches and listens closely. The only thing he can hear is the sound of his own breathing in and out. His breath is short and shallow. With his hands shaking, he fears he wouldn't be able to hit anything even if he had to shoot. *Damn Steven, pull yourself together.* He draws in a long breath, and then lets it out slowly. He repeats the deep breaths a few more times and tries his best to steady his trembling hands.

Soon, Robert steps back out of the house and signals for Steven to join him inside. Steven obeys and slowly, quietly makes his way through the trees toward the door. Deputy Evan's house isn't much of a house at all. It's barely bigger than the shed he and his friends have built in the woods. There isn't a kitchen, just a corner with a sink in the living room. There's a closet built off the opposite wall, with nothing in it but an old wooden outhouse style toilet. There is no tub, and no bed. There's a couch and a chair with a tiny table. There are stacks and stacks of paper on and underneath it.

Steven and his father look around in disbelief as they study all the pages posted to the old rotten wooden walls.

"Keep your ears peeled, son. He could be close."

They walk around the one room home. *It's built out of the same old wood and strips of tin as the underground bunker*, thinks Steven. He wonders how no one else has noticed such a big detail, especially the Sheriff who spends day after day working with this pig.

The Sheriff has to have seen that this is where his Deputy lives, God knows how many times. *How is it possible that he's never been inside?* Each paper on the wall has sketches of women. They're drawn being hung by their hands and stabbed. They're drawn being hung by their feet with their heads sliced off. And more, much more. Next to each sketch of a woman being killed are several of them before they were murdered. They're all beautiful and young girls with their hair done and their faces flawless.

Robert paces the floors looking at all the pictures... until he finds her. Steven looks over just as his father drops to his knees, and buries his face in his hands. Hung on the wall in front of Mr. Smith are several sketches of Ruth Ann. There are pictures drawn of her smiling and laughing. There's even one of her sitting with Robert on a swing that hangs from the branch of a giant oak tree. In the middle of all the pictures full of life and happiness, there's a lone sketch. Ruth Ann's head had been cut off and set away from the rest of her body that was in flames. Evan had drawn the image in such detail, he even had a tear drawn streaming down the face of her detached head.

Steven doesn't know what to say to his father. There are no words to comfort this grieving man. After all these years, he's finally found the killer of his lost sister. He now knows the way she died and why her body was never found. The sketch displays her on fire next to a body of water. There's a shovel in the picture, leaned against a tree just behind the flames.

"It looks like that lake by Johnston town. The one we used to go fishing at when I was little." Steven observes. "I wonder if he buried her there?"

Steven places his hand on his father's shoulder, but doesn't linger long. He turns his back to give Mr. Smith a moment of space to grieve. Steven walks over to the small table and picks up the stack of drawings on it. He gasps and drops the pages no quicker than he picked them up. His legs instantly numb, and his vision blurs. Now, scattered all over the dirty floor is sketch after sketch of Chloe Mead.

CHAPTER ELEVEN

Michael has been pacing the floor of their living room for the last hour. They've been waiting for Steven to show up with any sort of information on his dad all day. He and Chloe's worries are even starting to wear off onto John and their mother. Chloe has maintained her eerie feeling since they left the Smith home this morning. She can't seem to push away the images of all the girls in the newspapers. She wonders if Mr. Smith would turn on his own son, had he found out the secret.

Michael and Chloe are both convinced that Mr. Smith is the one who killed Misty, especially after stewing on it all day. It is the only thing that makes any sense. He had all the weapons that were used on the murdered girls years ago, he's kept all the newspapers, he has a temper and a drinking problem, and to top it all off he's losing his house. If anyone has a reason to snap, its Steven's dad.

Chloe has never been so scared in her life. She's also convinced that if anything happens to Steven, it'll be their fault for leaving him alone with the killer. Chloe and John sit on the couch watching Michael wear a trail on the wooden floor. Back and forth he storms, mumbling to himself. Once in a while they can understand a word or two that comes out of his mouth. Chloe catches a *"piece of shit"*, an *"All my fault"*, and a *"What am I going to do?"*. everything else that Michael's says is incomprehensible.

"Michael, I think we better go check it out," John says.

After a couple days of lying around to heal, John is finally able to walk short distances. He's been restless and feels like he needs to help. Not only has he wanted to find the killer before the lawmen point a finger at any of them, but he wants more than anything to avenge Misty's death. Just like everyone else, he wants to see justice brought to her killer.

Chloe slowly approaches the, now still, Michael. He's standing by the kitchen doorway staring blankly at his hurt brother.

"We have to go make sure Steven is okay," she says quietly as she slides her hand into his.

It's like talking to an injured animal, no sudden movements, Chloe thinks. Michael has been pacing and mumbling for long enough now, that his brother and girlfriend think he's lost it. Michael shakes the crazy thoughts from his head and nods in agreement. He doesn't understand why Chloe is talking to him like she's frightened of what to say, or even why John has been watching him with such a confused crease in his brow. *I must look like a lunatic,* he realizes.

Just as Chloe reaches for the door, there is a knock on it. They open it to find Sheriff Black standing on the porch, and two lawmen behind him on their horses. The sober look on their faces is bone chilling. The Sheriff is standing closely enough that Chloe can smell the onion on his breath the very second he opens his mouth to talk.

"Well," he says, "You're gunna' have to come with me, John. We know you did it."

His voice is loud, confident and controlled. He takes John by the arm, and forces him through the doorway. John winces in pain as Sheriff Black shoves him next to one of the horses. The Lawman sitting on it slips a rope around John's neck, and the Sheriff ties his arms behind his back.

"We found your name carved in two knife handles, as well as

the stock of a rifle in that shed, John." The Sheriff is now yelling and shoving a finger into John's chest. "We know that stuff is yours."

"NO!" Chloe yells, following them out to the road. "He didn't do it! It was Mr. Smith. Robert is the one who killed Misty!" She cries and pleads with the Sheriff. He only pushes her away and climbs back onto Ol' blue.

"You can't take him," Michael joins in the plea. "He can hardly even walk"

"We're gunna take him, and by tomorrow night we're gunna hang him," States the largest of the lawmen. "That Ol' Robert Smith didn't do anything wrong girl, we know it was your friend and we'll hang him after his trial in the morning."

The man steps off his horse and hands the reins over to another man in the circle. Before shoving Michael out of his way, he adjusts his belt, wiggling it up over the top of his belly roll. Then he storms past them all, and into the house. Michael follows after him, begging for his brother's life.

"You'd better shut your mouth, boy, or you'll be hanging right next to him. You may anyway, soon enough." he sneers. "It's only a matter of time, before we find proof that you're just as guilty as your twisted brother."

One room at a time he searches their home. The man looks thoroughly underneath furniture, in all the kitchen cupboards, and lastly in the bedrooms. Mrs. Hounds can hear all the commotion from her bedroom. She's too sick to move, and can speak no louder than a whisper, rendering her cries mute.

"Lookie here!" The man shouts as he pulls a photograph of Misty from underneath John's mattress. "I knew we'd find something in here."

Michael stands motionless in the bedroom doorway, all color drained from his face.

"Well boy, did you have something to do with all of this too? Or was it just your brother here who killed the girl?"

"Neither one of us sir, I swear to God. That picture is there because my brother loved Misty. He's innocent."

"We'll see about that. We're taking your brother now and if that Crawl girl's father decides you need to be locked up next to him, well come for you later."

The man shoves Michael into the wall with his shoulder in passing. Before he's completely out of the room he says in a cold voice directly in Michael's his ear, "Don't leave town either boy, I'll personally hunt you down."

The men make John walk for a few yards behind their horses. He is too slow moving, and his limp is far too prominent. He falls flat on his face and is dragged a couple of feet. Sheriff Black jumps off Ol' Blue and gives John one swift kick to the ribs before scooping him up. Several rocks are now embedded in the side of his face and its dripping blood. His clothes are torn and hanging from his body. He yells back to his brother and Chloe as the Sheriff tosses him onto the back of his horse.

"You have to find Steven," John shouts. "You have to make sure he's okay."

Sheriff Black taps Ol' blue with the spur on his boot heel, and with a couple of whoops and whistles the crew takes off in a quick jog back toward town. The men follow the Sheriff's lead and they're all soon out of sight. Michael and Chloe stand temporarily dumbfounded. Michael especially, is in shock and unable to speak. If he were to fight then they'd take him right along with his brother. And, if that were to happen then there'd be no one to uncover Mr. Smith.

"Whatever we do, it better be fast, Michael." Says Chloe.

"I know, we have to find Steven... now."

Michael storms to the car and starts the engine, leaving Chloe to chase after him. Chloe jumps in and slams the door shut, just as Michael starts pulling down the road. Chloe is unsure what to say to Michael. This is a horrible situation, and they're now in an actual relationship, it seems there are no words of comfort to be given. She looks over at the unreadable, determined look on his face, and can feel his pain in every part of her.

The first thing they notice when they pull into Steven's driveway, is that the car still isn't home.

"I wonder if either of them ever left?" Chloe asks.

"Stay close at my side."

Michael jumps out of the car and speeds for the house. Chloe runs after him, following instructions to stay close, trying her best to keep up without stepping on his heels. Michael pounds on the door with a closed fist.

"Open the door!" he shouts.

Michael only waits a few minutes before he kicks the door open. He stands in the doorway and yells again.

"I know you did it, ass hole! Where is Steven?"

Michael grabs a candlestick that's sitting on an end table just inside the door. He's decided spur of the moment that he's going to bash Mr. Smith in the head with it before he has a chance to strike first. It's the first possible weapon in sight, *it'll have to do*, he thinks.

Michael stomps from room to room looking for Steven or his father, with Chloe close in toe. There's no response to his calls and the house is eerily empty. The kitchen floor is covered in the newspapers from the basement. After a full sweep through of the house, Chloe and Michael stand over the papers and stare for a few moments, taking it all in.

"What a sick pig," Michael says.

He checks the basement last, but there's still no sign of Robert or Steven.

"I wonder where they went?" Chloe asks. " God, I hope Steven is okay."

"I don't know, Chloe. I don't know what to think about anything anymore. We have to find 'um both and get John out of trouble before tomorrow or he'll be hung and there's nothing we can do about it.".

Michael clears the lump from his throat, and wipes a tear from his cheek. Chloe has never seen Michael cry, and she's never been the type of girl to offer comfort. Up until the last few days, she could count on one hand how many times she's shed tears of her own. Chloe reaches her hands up to Michael's face and slips her palms around his cheeks. He drops his forehead to hers and breathes in every ounce of comfort he can suck from her.

Michael runs his warm hands up Chloe's body. He starts at her waist, and slowly works his way over the curves of her back, past her neck, and lastly down her arms. He stops at her hands, but only for a moment before letting his fingers work themselves into fists through his hair. Balling them in knots while he gasps for air. Michael forces his eyes open through the tears and allows his gaze to find Chloe.

"You have to be strong, Michael. For me and for John."

Chloe leans forward and presses her lips softly against his. She can taste the salt from his tears on her mouth. When she finally pulls away Michael takes in a deep breath and slowly nods. Keeping eye contact, Chloe's hands run from the sides of Michael's face, down his arms that are now lifeless at his sides, and intertwines them tightly in his fingers. They look around once more at the mess of papers all over their friend's kitchen floor.

"All of our guns were in that shed, the bows too." Michael says.

He doesn't know what to do if they get into a bind. He wants to be prepared and knows a candlestick might not get the job done.

"My dad has a brand-new revolver in his office. I saw it when I was lookin' for my skinnin' knife a couple months ago."

Michael thinks about it for a moment, mulling over the possibilities, trying to throw together a plan. They're grasping at straws, and don't even know where to start in looking for Robert and Steven.

"We could come back here, hide outside, and wait for Steven's father to come back."

"That could work," Chloe agrees. "It's worth a shot."

Michael and Chloe hurry back to the car. Stealing her father's gun is at least something. They're desperate, and sitting around doing nothing isn't an option. On the drive, they try to set some sort of a plan in motion. Perhaps they could take Robert Smith to the courthouse. Maybe if he sees John in custody, he'd confess and hand himself over. Something has to work, Michael thinks, we have to do something to make them set John free.

Chloe agrees to everything. She's doubtful, but willing to try. She finally feels like there's some sort of hope for John. She tries not to imagine what John's going through, sitting in the jailhouse with all the lawmen accusing him of murder. She's hopeful that since he's already received a beating, only days before, that maybe they'll leave him alone. She can still see him in her head, being dragged down the road by horses. Michael drives silently, remembering the same image.

"Wait here," says Chloe. "It'll only take me a few minutes, and I don't want Rosa tryin' ta talk to ya. There's just something about you Michael that really seems to bring the English out in her."

Chloe flashes him an inkling of smile with just one side of her face. This is the first hint of humor out of either of them since they'd woken up in each other's arms this morning. Michael molds his face into a smile back at her. It's a smile that's tainted with anxiety. He loves Chloe's smirk and can't help but appreciate her attempt at comfort. He watches Chloe closely as she runs to the house and disappears behind the giant door.

She lets it slam behind her and yells up the stairway.

"Rosa?"

Chloe hollers at every angle into the house as she walks to the office. There's no response, so Chloe assumes it's safe to pick the lock to her father's office without being seen. *Rosa must be outback or sleeping upstairs*, she thinks. She pulls a couple of clips out of her hair and bends them into a tool. Chloe has made it a habit to stick the clips into her pony-tail, even though she rarely needs them for her hair. It's a bit of a habit, she's always prepared. Chloe no longer gives it a second thought, and rarely even notices as she slides them into her hair each day.

The door clicks open in no time at all, and she lets herself in. Chloe slides open the top drawer of her father's desk, and moves aside a couple of papers to reveal a nice new shiny handgun. There are bullets in a small box next to it that have never been opened. Chloe loads the gun, one bullet at a time, before slipping the revolver it into the back of her jeans. She closes the desk drawer and walks back out of the room, relocking it behind her. Then she yells a few more times for Rosa, again with no response.

Chloe's only taken a few steps into the extended hallway when all of a sudden, a giant hand clamps over her mouth, and a strong arm quickly snakes around her waist. She's picked up off the ground and unable to think or breathe. She kicks her legs vigorously, and tries, without success, to reach for the gun. Her arms are held too tight against the sides of her body for her to be able to reach behind her back.

"No, you don't, sweet girl." The voice whispers in her ear.

The man's breath is foul enough for Chloe to smell it even with her nose and mouth covered. As soon as the scratchy voice sounds, she recognizes who it belongs to... Deputy Evan.

Chloe becomes quickly light headed, she's unable to take a breath. Her eyes are beginning to close and the muscles in her body are losing movement. Soon, Chloe is unconscious, in the arms of evil. He tosses her limp body over his shoulder and climbs the stairs up into her bedroom. The door has been left wide open into her bathroom, where he has Rosa tied up and gagged on the tile floor.

He slips Chloe out of her clothes, down to her undies, and then tosses one of Michael's old tee-shirts on her in their place. Evan smirks to himself at how clever he is. *This'll be a nice touch for that Hounds boy*, he thinks. Evan sets Chloe's still unconscious body down on a chair in the corner of her room, right next to her unused makeup stand. Chloe's mother insisted on her having a place to do her makeup in case she ever decided to make herself beautiful. Chloe had told her mother at the time that it was a waste of money and that she'd never be so shallow as to worry so much about her outer appearance. Until this very moment, this entire corner of the room has been unused.

Chloe wakes up to the disgusting smell of Evan. In a sudden

panic, she struggles to get away while he finishes tying her legs and waist to the chair. Her thrashing does no good. There's a thick cloth gag over her mouth. She is completely aware of what was going on, and there's nothing she can do about it. Chloe tries and tries to yell for help, but all that can be heard is muffles from the back of her throat. She thinks about Michael, sitting right outside of her house completely oblivious as to what's going on. She tries again to wiggle out of the ropes and scream. Chloe is still unable to do either, and is tiring quickly.

"Save your strength, girl."

A sleezy grin slowly spreads across Evan's face as he speaks. He seems to be proud of himself, excited even. There's a glimmer of joy in his eyes. The odor filling Chloe's entire bedroom is becoming unbearable. Her eyes water and her muscles are growing increasingly tired. A single tear runs down Chloe's face, as Evan lifts her in the chair and carries her to the doorway of the bathroom.

"Here," he says, while looking back and forth between her and Rosa. "Now you have a perfect view. I came here for you, but this extra beautiful lady sure is a nice surprise."

Evan stands next to Chloe with his arms folded. He admires the view of Rosa tied up and gagged on the floor.

Chloe again screams into her gag, but no sound comes through. She tries to move her body back and forth to make the chair slide or clank against the floor, but the heavy chair won't budge. Chloe is forced to sit there helplessly and watch as Evan makes his move on Rosa first.

Evan grabs a long, serrated blade that he had sitting on the counter. He kneels down a few inches from Rosa, and picks up her head by the back of her hair. Chloe shuts her eyes tight as not to see what's about to happen. Evan speaks to her in a steady, promising voice.

"I want you to watch everything, Miss Mead. Don't close your eyes, honey, or I will cut hers out."

Chloe opens her eyes. They're blurred, luckily, so the image of

Evan and Rosa before her is distorted through the tears. Chloe is only able to make out Rosa's frame, as she kicks and struggles to escape his clutches. He holds the blade to Rosa's neck and whispers something into her ear. Chloe can't hear his words, but whatever he said has stilled her. He picks up her arms by the rope that's tied them together, and secures them tightly to a towel rack next to the bathtub.

Chloe's vision has cleared just enough to see the stream of blood running from Rosa's nose, as well as make out the shallow rise and fall of her chest in breath. Rosa pleads with her eyes and gasps for a decent breath, yet she refuses to let a peep escape her lips.

Without batting an eye, Evan begins cutting into her flesh. He starts with deep slice down each of her arms, from elbow to wrist. Then he digs a second set of slices down each of her legs, from hip to knee. Rosa pants and holds her breath, until her head rolls forward. She's unconscious, with growing pools of blood at either side of her. Once Evan is finished, he looks up at Chloe with a grin.

"I like to see a bit of blood before I actually kill a woman," he sneers. "Now that I have you both where I want you, I'd better go take care of your little boyfriend before he intrudes on our party."

He turns back to Rosa before he walks out, and says directly into her unconscious ear, just loud enough for Chloe to hear, "Don't worry sweetheart, you won't die right off. You two will have plenty of time together."

He then chuckles, turns for the door, and walks out.

Michael has been waiting in the car for what seems to him like a lifetime. Chloe said she'd be in and out, but it's taking her a while and he's starting to worry. He's seen her pick lock after lock, and knows for a fact it's never taken her this long. At first, he assumed that Rosa wouldn't let her past that easily. Maybe Chloe had to distract her, or talk to her before sneaking to the office door with ill intentions. Now, there's something nagging at the back of Michael's mind telling him that something has gone sour. After a small debate within himself, he decides that he'd better go in and check things out. They're in a hurry and he's running on fumes as it is.

Michael lets himself into Mead house. He goes straight for the office first. Michael doesn't yell for Chloe or for Rosa. The house seems too empty, too quiet for that. Up until a couple days ago, Michael insisted on waiting in the entry way for her, or he was by her side. Everything about today feels different. He twists the handle to the office door, and it is locked. He knocks, and waits a few moments for a response, but there's nothing.

Next, he lets himself into the kitchen. Just around the corner from the kitchen entryway, he stops. On high alert he listens closely for the sound of anyone talking. Only silence greets him, so he makes the turn into the room. It's an utter disaster. Tomatoes, carrots, and salad are strewn across an entire counter along with the floor. There are also a few chairs that have been tipped over, and a picture knocked off a wall. Panicked, Michael yells Chloe's name. He runs out of the room and up the stairs.

Just as he twists the handle to Chloe's room, the Ex-Deputy Evan jumps out from behind a door on the other side of the hall, with base-ball bat. He slams Michael in the head with one swift blow. The sudden contact with the wood knocks him out cold. Evan expected Michael to check Chloe's room when she never returned to the car. He's been hiding in wait for the perfect opportunity to bash Michael from behind.

This isn't the first time Evan has knocked out Michael Hounds by surprise.

This is, however, a first for Evan in other ways. He's never been able to torture three people at once, and is contemplating on his approach. Evan positions Michael against the wall so he'll have a clear view of Chloe when he wakes up. This way he'll be able to see Chloe's pain as she watches him kill Rosa first. Like a ripple effect. Evan puts the gun he retrieved from Chloe's belt on the edge of her bed. He wants Michael to see it and not be able to reach it.

Evan grins proudly at Chloe as he fastens thick ropes around Michael. He starts tying Michael's wrists to his ankles, leaving his body hunched over at the middle. Then he ties a separate rope around Michael's chest, up under his armpits and fastens it to a heavy wooden chest against the wall. One thing Evans prides himself on, is his ability to tie an undoable knot.

Only once has anyone escaped the clutches of Deputy Evan, and that was years before in this same town. He had a girl tied up in his home, hanging limp from the ceiling rafters, bleeding out. He'd held her hostage for a full day and inflicted a new stab wound on her limp body periodically over time. He'd left to get some food, and when he returned home, she was gone. Apparently. she was a bit more lively than he thought when he'd left the house. He grabbed a stick of dynamite and followed her blood trail all the way to the clinic. After spotting her through a window, he lit the stick, tossed it in, and ran. Evan waited a few weeks to make sure that no one suspected him of the murder before he left town.

Evan didn't return to the area until a job opened up as Deputy. At the time, he was excited to take the job. He couldn't wait to check up on and watch the families of the girls he had killed years before. Evan enjoys seeing how his deeds have torn families apart. Evan has been killing girls across the country for years. He killed his first victim when he was 20 years old, and over time it's become an addiction. Like an unstoppable impulse.

Sometimes Evan will -stalk a girl for months before making a move. Such has been the case with both Misty Crawl, and Chloe Mead. Rosa and Michael are merely caught in the crossfire. Nothing more than welcome inconveniences to Evan's original intentions. Evan now holds their lives in his hands, and he can feel the power building up within him. He walks first to Chloe and puts his hands around each side of her face. He holds her head straight forward and points it at Rosa.

"You keep watching my work on your friend. I want to save you for later." He hisses.

The blood has spread all over the floor. Rosa's chest continues to rise and fall in shallow breaths, as the life is draining out of her. Evan reaches around the door to grab something from a large black duffel bag that until now has been blocked from Chloe's sight. He pulls out a jar and sets it on Chloe's lap. Chloe looks down and instantly panics, trying with all she's worth to squeal and break free of her restraints.

She screams into her gag at the top of her lungs, but no sound escapes into the room. The jar on Chloe's lap is filled to the brim with the toes of Evans victims. They're each a different color of brown and black from rotting over the years in a jar. Many of the toes still have paint on the nails. Sitting on the very top is a fresh, small pinky toe with purple paint neatly covering the tip. It's the same color of purple as the flowers on Misty's dress.

CHAPTER TWELVE

Steve and his father make their way slowly and quietly through the woods back to town. Robert leads the way, backtracking first as to enter on the main road as if they've been walking from home.

"I think we should go straight to Sheriff Black, and then go find Chloe," Steven whispers to his father as they creep through the trees.

"NO!"

Robert snaps at his son almost as quickly as the statement came out. Mr. Smith wants to get to Evan before the law has a chance to. He's been dreaming about catching his sister's abductor and isn't about to pass up his chance. The only reason to make any stops in town now would be to fill a gas can. The sketch of Robert's sister's body in flames, burns bright in mind. He's now contemplating on doing the same to Deputy Evan once he's found.

If Evan is arrested, he'll most likely be hanged after a speedy trial, and that isn't enough for Robert Smith, not by a long shot. Mr. Smith wants Evan to feel the pain he's inflicted on so many women. If he has any say at all, then Evan can't get away with a mere hanging. Unless Robert is the one personally holding the hanging rope, he'll never be satisfied.

"We'll save your friend, son, if she isn't already dead. But that man needs to pay for what he's done. The law just isn't going to give him what he deserves."

Steven cringes at the thought of his father unleashing his anger on the man who killed one of his own family members. Hateful energy radiates off Mr. Smith. Steven shuts his mouth and doesn't push the matter any further. All he can do is follow his father, and pray in his mind that Chloe is safe. The only comforting thought Steven can pull from the depths of his mind's chaos is that Michael will likely be keeping Chloe within arm's length at all times.

"I think we should go to the Hounds' house first and see if Chloe is there. She don't like to be home, and if they're all there then we will have some help in finding and catching Evan." Steven says as they near the road to enter town.

"Okay." His father agrees without argument.

Just as they step onto the main road, a gang of lawmen gallop towards them on their horses.

"Stay calm." Mr. Smith advises.

He seems to be talking more to himself than to Steven. Steven glances at his father, and can tell right off that he's struggling to steadying his breath. Robert wipes the palms of his hands on his jeans. Steven follows his father's lead and convinces himself not to give anything away. They continue to walk steadily, but slow their pace in order to make contact with the lawmen gaining ground on them.

Sheriff Black leads the crew, and he pulls his horse to a halt once they approach Steven and his father. John is draped over the back of Ol' Blue. His hands are tied together by a rope. The rope is then attached to his neck along with the saddle. His face is bloodied, and his clouded eyes meet Steven's. John sighs a breath of relief to see his friend is alive and well, then he allows his head drop in defeat.

"What are you doing with the boy?" Asks Mr. Smith.

"We found his name written all over the contraband in that shed in the woods. When we went to pick him up, he had a picture of the victim hidden under his bed." The Sheriff tells him.

John wiggles and groans before he shouts to his friend.

"Tell them, Steven! Tell them about the bows and all the shit we took from your basement. Tell them about how your dad has all those newspapers."

John struggles, trying to loosen the rope from around his wrists. He pleads to his friend for help.

"Shut up, boy." The same lawman who searched his house, leans over to Ol' Blue. He thumps John on the back of the head with his pistol. John goes instantly limp, slumped over the butt of the horse.

Sheriff Black takes a long look at Robert Smith, recalling his odd behavior the day they found Misty's body.

"Do either of you have anything to say for yourselves?" He asks. "This Hounds boy has been ranting on and on about you since we left his house."

The Sheriff keeps his eyes on Mr. Smith. He's been suspicious of Robert since they were alone together in the woods. Everything that John has been saying is actually starting to make sense to him, though he's refused to say it out loud to the other men in his crew.

All of the other lawmen at his side are very hell bound on hanging John Hounds, and being finished with the whole mess. The sheriff is well aware that if there were actually a reason to investigate Robert Smith, he'd have to face it on his own. Sheriff Black thinks of the distant and chilling look in Robert's eyes that he'd personally witnessed, as well as the beating that he had already given the Hounds boy for really no reason at all. Sheriff Black sits back on his horse, waiting on a response from Mr. Smith.

"I do have newspaper clippings from years ago, and one of those clippings tell all about my sister. You remember her, don't you Sheriff?"

Mr. Smith's words cut right through the Sheriff. None of the other men on their horses behind the Sheriff were around when all the killings took place, but they've heard the stories, especially now amidst the chaos of it all.

"Ruth Ann was her name, and she was never found. I've kept the papers all these years hoping that your men wouldn't give up and would find her abductor. But you never did. And, now you have this young boy in custody. Why in the hell would you accuse such a young boy of the new crime? You all think it's the same old killer from before, you just don't dare actually say the words. You don't dare admit to yourselves that you 'men of the law' never actually found him."

Mr. Smith stands his ground, allowing himself to rant and rave. He stands up to Sheriff Black, letting his anger loose, all the while being careful not to say anything that would give away himself or his own motive or plans.

"You'd better mind your tongue, Robert Smith!" Sheriff Black is clearly upset. Of course he remembers Ruth Ann. Either way, he refuses to let a simple store clerk speak to him this way. "Let's go men, before we have to arrest an innocent man for losing his temper on a Sheriff."

He kicks the side of his horse softly and flips the rains. The men trot off together to the jailhouse, with a limp John on the back of Ol' Blue. Steven and his father watch as they ride away, leaving them quietly on the side of the road.

"Thanks for not saying anything, Steven, I promise we'll try to find your friend."

"Yeah," he mumbles back.

Mr. Smith realizes that his son doesn't agree with the way they're going about things. He also realizes that all Steven had to do was mention all of the sketches in Evan's pigsty of a home, and it would all be over... but he didn't. Mr. Smith is grateful to his son for being supportive of his revenge on Ruth Ann's Killer.

"We better hurry before John wakes back up and gives the lawmen motivation to beat him, or even move to a quicker hangin'" Robert says.

"Yeah."

Steven drops his chin to his chest and follows his dad. The two of them walk into town and toward the car at the store as fast as they can, trying their best not to look suspicious. Mr. Smith made his final decision against purchasing a gas can. The last thing he wants right now is to be stuck in conversation with his boss' nosy wife, especially after the drunken episode he subjected her to this morning. He's also assuming that the Sheriff, or his men, could show up at his house anytime tonight for another chat, so whatever had to be done with Evan, had to be done tonight.

Steven climbs into the passenger seat and quickly catches his breath.

"I hope Michael and Chloe are okay."

Steven stares blankly out the window and thinks of all the drawings of Chloe in Evan's home. There must have been dozens of them. They're mostly all drawn of her sleeping, which Steven thinks is strange. He wondered if Evan has snuck into Chloe's house and watched her sleep, or if he just imagined her room and the faces she pulls while dreaming. He shudders at the thought.

With the town soon in the rear-view mirror, Mr. Smith presses the gas pedal nearly through the floorboard. He's on a mission to save his son's friend, and to unleash the hatred that's been pent up for all these years. Anxiety is near the consuming point for Steven, it's a feeling he can't escape, like an inner buzz that's swallowing him whole. He's worried to the point of tears, which doesn't go unnoticed by his dad. Neither of them says a word about it. Their silence remains unbroken until the car is parked in the Hounds' driveway.

"Son, I know that I already told you how important it is that you don't freeze up. But I feel like you need to hear it again."

Steven's father sounds surprisingly focused and mellow. *The calm before the storm*, Steven thinks. Robert continues to instruct his son.

"We'll need to watch each other's back. Once we have that

bastard secured somewhere, I want you to walk away, boy... do you hear me?"

Mr. Smith doesn't take his eyes off the steering wheel. He's in a trance, thinking about what he'll do and say to Evan. He doesn't want Steven to be around for it. Although Robert has lost his temper on Steven in the past, he's always prided himself on being a good father. nearly all of the men he knows have taken a belt to their kids at some point or another, 'to teach them a lesson', they say.

Robert hated himself for it every time, *but it's all a part of being a parent,* he thinks. The last time he tried for weeks to convince himself that it was the best thing, but deep down he knows better. Mr. Smith finally looks over to take a close look at his son. Steven is almost a grown man. He's strong in stature, much like himself, but with a much more innocent heart. What he'd witnessed with Misty could have been enough to break him, but seeing his own dad do the horrible things he intended will most definitely push him over the edge.

"You know that I love you, Steven," He finally says. "I'm sorry if I haven't been the father you deserved your whole life, and I'm sorry I couldn't make things work out with your mother when you were young."

Robert feels the need to make amends with anything that may be hanging over their heads as father and son. He has to make every-thing right before they throw themselves into the path of a demented killer.

"I love you too dad," Steven replies flatly.

Steven's never held anything against his father. He knows to steer clear of his dad when there's alcohol involved, but other than that, they usually get along quite well.

Steven avoids eye contact, he's afraid and compliant. Briefly he wonders about his aunt. She and his father must have been close for him to react the way he had years ago when she went missing. A deeper understanding of his father has branched inside of him. The hatred his father carries on his back makes sense. There is no judgement on Steven's part for his father wanting to get his hands on Evan, only fear.

They look around in the trees and to the sides of the home before knocking on the door. Evan could be hiding around any corner, and they'll leave no stone unturned. He'll likely be following Chloe wherever she is, and that includes John and Michael's house. Robert can feel it deep in his bones, that once they find Chloe, Evan will be close by.

It takes what seems like an eternity for Mrs. Hounds to open the door. Her eyes are red and puffy, and she's holding a towel that's nearly soaked through with blood. The stress and cries for John have sent her cough into overdrive. She's lost a few more pounds in just a couple days. She's frail and her legs are shaking. Without a word, she swings the door open wide to let them in, and then returns to her seat on the couch. She looks at Steven with fresh tears forming in her eyes.

"They took John. They think he did it."

"We saw him ma'am," Steven tells her, and hangs his head in shame. "On the back of Sheriff Black's horse."

Guilt swirls in Steven's guts over the fact that John is still in the clutches of the nasty old Sheriff. He could have easily been the hero who revealed the true killer and set his friend free. But instead here he is, sitting on John's couch and watching his sick mother fall apart. He is keeping the secret merely for his father's satisfaction of revenge, and the truth of it makes him sick.

Mr. Smith also feels the depth of their guilt in secrecy. He hadn't fully realized the pain that he himself was causing others, to fulfill his own hidden agenda. Deep down he knows that the pain and stress of this whole mess could easily kill this fragile woman. *At what cost are his actions justified?* he wonders, though he remains utterly determined to follow through.

"We won't let them hurt your son." Robert makes her a tainted promise. "Do you know were Michael and Chloe are? We need to find them, so we can work together and help John."

Steven looks over at his father in shock. *How could he be so calm? How could he not tell her that we know Deputy Evan is after Chloe?* A part of Steven thought he was figuring his father out, until now. The lies and secrecy are too much, he's nauseous, and breaking out in a cold sweat. Steven watches in disbelief as his father places his hand on Mrs. Hounds' knee waiting for a response.

"I don't know. They left when Sheriff Black took John. They didn't say a word to me they just sped away. I couldn't even get out of bed to stop them." Mrs. Hounds stares at the floor, tears streaming. "I couldn't help my boys," she sobbed in regret.

Mrs. Hounds is dying fast, and she knows it. She's prays that she'll at least live to see both of her sons back home, safe and alive through this mess. She could pass any time, any day. With one in custody facing a hanging, and the other out searching for a killer, the odds of her seeing them both again with a breath in their lungs slim. Too slim. If things don't turn around for the Hounds boys, and fast, she won't survive it.

As Mr. Smith attempts to offer her a little comfort, Steven disappears into the kitchen to compose himself. He comes back with a glass of water and some bread for Mrs. Hounds.

"You should eat Ma'am, we'll go and look for Michael."

She only nods, keeping her eyes fixated on the floor. Mr. Smith stands over Mrs. Hounds for a few moments, holding her hand gently. For those anxious moments he doesn't want to leave her alone, neither does Steven, but they have to.

"Do you need anything before we go?" Steven asks, kneeling by her side.

"No Steven, just go help my boys, please. You have to help them out of this mess."

"Yes, ma'am."

Steven and his father make another loop around the house, searching the yard and the surrounding trees, searching one last time for any sign that Evan may have been there. They're unable to find anything.

"I wonder if they went to our house." Steven questions.

"I don't think going back to our house is the best idea, son. Not yet, and not unless we have to. Who knows if John's convinced the Sheriff to go poking around? We can't risk being taken in alongside him, not unless we're completely out of other options." Robert says, scratching at his chin nervously. "You said Chloe doesn't like being home... but do you think maybe they'd go there anyway?" He asks. "I think it's worth a shot. At least to check."

"I guess it won't hurt to look." Steven agrees. He's willing to look anywhere, and do anything to help his friends. Steven is growing more and more afraid for Chloe's life by the minute. Seeing his friend's mom in such despair put things in a whole different light. Everything is sinking in all at once, he can feel the reality of it all in the pit of his stomach. Another wave of nausea takes over his body, and he feels like he's going to throw up.

It's a short drive to Chloe's house. Her car is parked in front of the house. A giant flow of relief streams through Steven at the site of it. But it doesn't add up. Something doesn't seem right. With Michael's mom in her condition, and John being thrown in the middle of this awful situation, why on earth would they be at Chloe's house? Steven can feel something's wrong.

"Wait, dad," Steven says as his father opens the door to get out. "Something is wrong. They wouldn't just be hanging out here." Steven speaks with caution.

The front door is wide open, and the silence in the giant home is paralyzing. Steven and his father draw their pistols, and slowly make their way from room to room. There's nothing on the first floor except the messy kitchen, clearly disturbed.

"Something happened in here Steven, you're right." Robert whispers to his son as they continue their sweep through.

They make for the stairs, ready to take a shot at any moment. The rooms are empty... all but Chloe's. They can hear someone moving around on the other side of her bed as soon as they open the door to peak in. Cautiously, they find Michael, tied up with his head down.

He's sobbing, hardly able to catch a breath. He jumps at the site of Steven and his father. Once he realizes who's there, he begins to thrash at his restraints and yells.

"Oh my God Steven, he took her! He took her! We have to get to them before he kills her!"

As Steven cuts the ropes off his friend's wrists and ankles, Mr. Smith finishes his sweep through. He opens the bathroom door that was left slightly cracked. His gun falls to the floor, and he drops to his knees. The sight is nearly too much for Mr. Smith to handle. Thought of Ruth Ann flashes before his eyes as he stares at what was left of Rosa.

Rosa's arms are still hanging from the towel rack, with only her torso attached. Her head is lying on the counter and her legs are in the tub. One of her feet has the toes cut off and they're spread out in the blood on the floor... guts pushed into a pile against the wall.

Michael joins Robert, then he wipes the snot from his face and the dampness from his eyes.

"He made her watch. He made Chloe watch and he took his time. He told her that she would be his best girl yet, and left with her." Michael recalls Evan's every word as he points at the floor. "He took off his shoes until he was ready to leave so he wouldn't leave any blood prints behind. I've never seen a man covered in so much blood."

CHAPTER THIRTEEN

John opens his eyes and looks around the dank jail cell. His hands are cuffed to the thick metal bars that are holding him in. He's sitting on the floor, propped up against the wall. The room is made up entirely of three other small cells, they're separated by the bars alone. The other cells are empty. John is completely alone, in excruciating pain, and afraid. He prays that Michael will be able to find some kind of proof that he's innocent. He's grateful that Michael isn't locked up next to him, it's the only hope he has to hold onto.

Sheriff Black mozies in, with Mr. Crawl at his heels.

"You have a visitor, boy," the Sheriff mumbles to John with his head hung low.

Mr. Crawl wraps his fist around the bars holding John. He's just out of reach, and John wonders if the Sheriff cuffed him to that particular bar by the wall for a reason. He's glad that he can't be reached by anyone who isn't in the cell with him. Only the lawmen have access to him physically. John locks eyes with Mr. Crawl, he has no reason to look away.

"I knew it was you," Mr. Crawl crouches down at the knees, so he's eye level with John. "I knew it was you all along, and you'll hang for what you did to my Misty." Tears take over his eyes, and Mr. Crawl takes a long look at what he believes to be the killer of his daughter. "Why? I *need* to know why you'd hurt her. She was perfect, and you took her from me." Tears run down his face in broken waves. He wipes the snot from below his nostrils and straightens his back. "We're finally going to bury her, now that you're caught. You'll never understand what it feels like to put your baby in the ground."

Mr. Crawl has so many things he wanted to say to his daughter's killer. Now that he is looking the accused in the eye, he draws a blank. Everything he'd planned on saying to John has faded away. The only thing that actually matters to Mr. Crawl now, is being able to take his daughters rotting body away from the jailhouse and put her to rest. He shakes his head and leaves the room.

"Wait," John begs, "I didn't do it, I'd never hurt her, I loved Misty."

His words fade into thin air. Mr. Crawl has no interest in hearing what John has to say. The grief of Misty's death has exhausted him. He doesn't stop to hear John out, nor does he pause once out of sight to listen in secrecy. The words fall on deaf ears. Now that he's seen John behind bars, and looked him in the eye, he feels it's finalized. The deed is done, there's no turning back, he can put his daughter to rest and try to find peace.

John continues to shout, proclaiming his innocence, in hopes that someone, anyone, outside the jailhouse might hear and show pity on him. He's sure that the longer he yells the worse his beatings may be, but he doesn't care. He has to do something. This could very well be his last day, and he'll be damned before he rolls over and gives up.

Sheriff Black is standing outside of the jail house with two lawmen on either side of him. Evening is rolling in and the town is preparing a funeral service for Misty. Her body has been sitting outside the jailhouse for days now. The hole to put her in has been prepared in the cemetery and her final resting place has been waiting to greet her. Now that they have her accused killer in custody, they're ready to lower her body underground.

The Sheriff shifts around on his feet, uneasy about arresting John Hounds. There are many others who also doubt his guilt, and presume him to be innocent. Most of them are keeping their mouths shut, focusing only on putting Misty to rest. Several of the townsfolk feel that as long as someone answers for Misty's murder, then they can put it all behind them, guilty or not. They're living in fear, and assume that they'll forever be doubtful no matter who actually pays the price for this heinous crime.

Sheriff Black listens to John screaming his innocence, while watching all of the familiar faces of his town gather and make their way to the cemetery. They can all hear his words, yet they turn the other cheek. He tilts his head and addresses one of the men at his side.

"They're only going to ignore him for so long," he says.

"Do you want me to go in and shut him up?" asks the man on is right.

"No, the kid's been through enough. I beat him too hard the other day. Besides, I'm starting to wonder if he's even the man we're looking for."

"You shouldn't let 'em get to you when they cry like that. They all do it, guilty or not, it happens every time." The man on his left says, while adjusting his belt.

"Well, I think I'm gunna' to head over to Robert Smith's place anyhow, just to check things out. Will ya' stick around, make sure no one else goes in?"

"Sure thing," the belt adjuster says. "It's your town, your prisoner, so I guess it's your say. I'd handle things a little different myself, but if this is what you want us to do... well, I suppose we'll stick to it."

Sheriff Black nods his head and leaves the two on post. All of the other lawmen have left, returning to their ranks in their hometowns. Only these two are left to help Sheriff Black control the situation, as well as deliver a sort of trial in the morning when a judge is due to arrive. Sheriff Black briefly wonders if he's done the right thing by firing Deputy Evan. They could use the extra hand, especially during a trial and likely hanging. On the other hand, he'd struggle to live with his own conscience if he were to leave Deputy Evan with John right now. It's a double-edged sword, lose all around.

He jumps on the back of Ol' Blue and rides off. He feels like he's missing something, like he's skipped something over, something important and can't he mentally place what it is. With John already in custody, and a judge on the way, there isn't much time to get his mind right. If something is off kilter, then it'll likely stay that way.

The Sheriff rides up to the Smith house and notices right of that the front door is wide open. The entire door is barely hanging from the hinges. Sheriff Black ties Ol' Blue to a pole of the porch, and draws his gun before going in.

Everything looks to be in its proper place, all except for the kitchen. The newspapers they'd discussed are strung about. They're covering the floor completely, and the table has been moved out of the room. Sheriff Black recalls the murdered women as he looks at all the circled articles. The first paper he picks up contains the entire story of a girl who'd been hung by a tree and shot with multiple arrows. The Sheriff shutters. He sets the paper back down and glances around the rest of them. Mr. Smith has underlined the dates on the papers as if they're significant. The Sheriff wonders why, and still can't seem to place the origin of his doubts.

I need to find Mr. Smith and ask him about the dates and why they were underlined, he thinks, maybe with some help and clarity he can figure out what he's mentally missing. By the looks of this kitchen, Mr. Smith is either involved, or may at least know who might be.

Like lightning it hits him. Sheriff Black gets a jolt of energy and excitement, with the realization that today he could uncover serial killer from years before. The one who'd slipped through not only his but several other men's fingertips. A man capable of the unthinkable. Not only does the life of John Hounds depend on him, but so does his own personal dignity and pride. This could be his chance to fill the void in his life, give him purpose and reason. A grin spreads across Sheriff Black's face as he leaves the Smith home on a mission.

The Sheriff rushes his horse past the Hounds and the Victors homes first, searching for Robert's car. He'd seen not too long ago that Steven was with him. They weren't at the funeral service, and neither were Michael or Chloe. He knows their faces well, and in light of John being locked away, their likely whereabouts is narrowed. The next house on his list is the Mead mansion. He gives Ol' blue a swift jolt to the flanks and runs him for all he's worth. A sigh of relief rushes through Sheriff Black as he rides up to the giant house. Both Chloe and Robert's cars are sitting in the driveway. *This is it*, he thinks, *I'm finally going to get the information I need to actually crack the case. To do something good in my life.*

Sheriff Black gives the door three stern knocks. He only waits a moment and then knocks again, even harder. There's still no answer. The Sheriff twists the unlocked handle and helps himself in.

"Hello?" he yells into the house. "Is there anyone here?"

He's greeted by more silence, the eerie kind, the sort that chills to the bone. Sheriff Black looks around the entryway and up the steps. There is fresh mud on the tiles heading up the stairs. He checks around every corner and listens closely for voices. The hair on the Sheriff's arms stand on end as he tip-toes up the steps, following the periodic mud chunks. A tale-tale sign that someone has been there, very recently.

As he reaches the top of the steps, he notices a baseball bat lying in the middle of the hallway. *Strange, and out of place*, he thinks. Everything else in this house seems to be in strict order. A place for everything and everything in its place. Slowly, he pulls back the hammer on his gun, and rounds the corner into Chloe's room. There's a chair tipped on its side in the middle of the room, and some cut apart rope all over the floor. There's a closed door in front of the chair with what appears to be blood seeping into the bedroom carpet from under the doorway. Sheriff Black hold his breath and opens it slowly.

As the door swings wide, he gasps and takes an involuntary step back. He trips and falls backward over the chair positioned in perfect view of a decapitated and mutilated body. The Sheriff scrambles, pulling himself back up to his feet. He holds his breath takes a good look at the head on the counter. He's never seen this woman, he's certain of that.

The blood on the floor is thickening, like gelatin. He can tell its fresh, but not quite fresh enough for still steady flow from the body parts. He guessed it to have happened over an hour ago, but it's just that... a guess. Every part of this woman has bled out. His mind snaps to John, and the time they'd taken him from his home. John Hounds had to have been in custody when this happened. This dead woman is proof that he's innocent.

"I knew it."

He runs from the room, down the steps and out of the house. He unties Ol' Blue in record time and speeds off to town.

The sky is starting to darken, and just as he suspected, a small mob is forming in front of the jailhouse. The friends and family of Misty Crawl are emotional, worked up from the service that commenced only minutes before. They're shouting at the lawmen that are standing their ground in front of the door. Each with a hand on their pistols, ready to fire if needed. Sheriff Black ties the rains to his horse, steps past the people onto the small porch in front of the door. Confidently, he holds up his hands to settle the crowd.

"John Hounds is telling the truth. He's innocent," the Sheriff shouts.

"How do you know?" An elderly man yells in a gruff voice from the back of the crowd.

"There's another body," he says a little quieter, and exhales a long breath.

The crowd stills. Some gasp.

"Who?" Mrs. Victor's voice cracks in fear.

"I don't know who she was, it was at the Mead residence, I'm guessing she was the help."

While giving the town a rundown of the goings on, and making a plan, the Sheriff can't help but to notice that the Ex-Deputy Evan isn't a part of it. He's assumed Evan to be upset, withdrawn even, but to miss out on all of this, he'd never. The Sheriff knows him too well for that. When the Sheriff had asked Evan to return his badge, he'd acted a bit oddly about it.

The Sheriff recalls the way Evan had a sly smile as he handed over his badge and walked away from the job without a word. As the Sheriff stands before the frightened and angry mob, he remembers how Evan had lived in his town years before when all of the previous murders took place. Everything about Evan floods into his memory, especially the inner workings of his demented demeanor over the years.

It really hits him... He'd left Misty's body out as bait, and hadn't even realized that he'd made the catch when Evan was poking around. He remembers years back, how everything had suddenly stopped about the time that Evan moved away. *How the hell could I miss this*, he wonders? He finishes addressing the public and then walks into the jailhouse for a moment to clear his head.

To his surprise, John is no longer yelling, but passed out on the floor in a small pool of blood. One of the lawmen shrugs.

"We couldn't handle his yelling, sir," he says.

John is still breathing. Sheriff Black lets out a sigh of relief that he's still alive. He unlocks the cuffs from John's wrists and lifts him up to a seated position against the wall.

"Let's hope he actually wakes back up while we're gone."

He shakes his head in disappointment, both to himself as well as the rest of the men who've managed to mess everything up. *No wonder the killer got away the first time*, he thinks. He looks around at his small posse. There are two lawmen and three young farmers, all ready to search the woods. Everyone else has given up, and retired to their homes to grieve. The farmers appear to be in their 20s. The Sheriff was not familiar with the younger crowd, and can only assume that they're relatives to the Crawl family.

He shakes the young men's hands, and thanks them for their help before filling everyone in on his suspicion of his Ex-Deputy.

John's eyes blur as they slowly open. He has a splitting headache and his hand is sitting in a warm pool of blood. He instantly reaches for the back of his head and can feel the open gash at the base of his hairline. His cheek also feels like it's on fire. As he runs a few fingers across his rocky flesh from being pulled behind the horse, he remembers why he's there. The second observation that comes with consciousness is that his wrists are no longer cuffed.

John focuses his sight on the light in front of him. It's the last sliver of daylight coming through a wide-open door. His heart makes a leap, and he struggles to stand. His knees give way beneath him, his weight is too much. John can hear the men talking in the room over about Deputy Evan and about another body being found. He sits back down, strains his ears, and focuses on their words.

John listens to Sheriff Black explain about how he found the body torn apart and cut into pieces, just like with Misty. John eavesdrops more to learn that both Chloe and Robert's cars are at the Mead place, but that the house is empty aside from the dead woman. Panic sets in as John thinks about his brother and Chloe. He closes his eyes and prays to God that they're alive.

Slowly, John rises to his feet, steadying himself against the wall on his way up. He's dizzy and covered in blood. He limps to the doorway close to him, following their voices. For a moment he stands in the doorway unnoticed. The men are utterly focused on Sheriff Black's story.

"Did you look through the rest of the house for my brother?" John finally asks, to their surprise.

Every man in the room jumps at the sound of his voice. They weren't expecting him to waken. The sudden unexpected voice scares the living daylights out of each of the men. He steadies his body and holds his weight with is hands on the doorway. His voice is hoarse and he's covered in rocks and blood. The belt adjusting lawman who had clocked John in the back of the head twice now, jumps up and out of his chair. He helps steady John and offers him the chair to sit on. He actually feels guilty for John's condition, which is somewhat rare. In part, he's responsible for this young man who's covered in both new and old blood.

"Son, you should sit down," he tells him. "Let me find someone to help get you cleaned up."

He steps out of the jailhouse, and within seconds he's pulling a woman in from the street to help take a look at John. She gasps at the sight of him, and quickly retreats to fetch some first aid supplies, towels and clothing.

"Well, Sheriff, do you know where my brother is?" John asks again.

He doesn't pay much attention to the other men in the room, be it those who've mistreated him, or the new faces. He's too worried about Michael, and about his friends for that matter. The last he'd seen his brother, it was mid-afternoon and they were headed out the door to find Steven. He glances over to the small barred window. It's starting to get dark.

"Well, what in the hell are you doing sitting here then?" John is upset, mind still full of fog. He's trying his best not to lose his temper. The pounding in his head has no room for that. He has no strength to stand or to yell, and his voice is almost completely gone. "You have to go and find them. You have to make sure that pig hasn't hurt any of them!" John is furious, and the vulnerable notion of helplessness is making it worse.

The Sheriff rises, "he is right men, we've wasted enough time discussing details."

The men follow him out in a determined huff, leaving John to wait on help for his wounds. The last man to walk out the door is the condescending lawman, the one without much to say. He turns back to John.

"That woman will help you boy, and then I suggest you go on home."

John holds his breath as he watches them leave, wishing he was of better use. He can see them outside, saddling up their horses and checking their guns. John tries again to stand and is still unable to hold his weight. He feels just as powerless as he had in the days before when everyone was searching for Misty. Only this time it's for his brother. John can't believe what's going on around him. He draws in a few deep breaths, slowly hoping to regain his strength some. Again, he tries to stand. His knees tremble, and his head is in a fuzz. He puts a hand on the back of the chair to steady himself, still trying to fully regain consciousness.

John doesn't want to sit back down, and he doesn't want to rest. He's growing more and more anxious by the minute. He's determined to help his brother, even if it kills him. *Michael would do the same for me, and I know it, which is probably why they're missing and in the mess they're in*, he thinks.

The short middle-aged woman rushes back into the room with towels, a bucket of water, a bottle of vodka and a small bag. She looks familiar, but John is still confused, he can't place who she is. He sits back down while the she lays everything out on the floor.

Her voice is shaking, "I'm so sorry they did this to you." She pulls a pair or tweezers out of the bag first. "This is going to hurt somethin' fierce, do you want anythin' to bite down on?" she asked.

"No ma'am, just please try to hurry." John mumbles before gripping the sides of his seat and tightening his jaw.

She dumps a large amount of the Vodka down the side of his face, and then takes a hefty swig of it. One rock at a time, she pulls them from his flesh, and the gash on the back of his neck takes four stitches. John hugs the chair to his chest and fights back the tears.

"These are the smallest clothes my husband has." She tells him once the bandages are all in place and the blood is wiped clean.

"Thank you."

She leaves them by the door, and apologizes again on the entire town's behalf.

John winces in pain, and dresses carefully, as not to disrupt his fresh bandages. He feels stronger on his feet than he did before. One foot at a time, he makes way for the fresh evening air, with each step he regains his balance along with his confidence and sense of freedom. It's quite nice to have the smell of Misty's rotting body gone. He only wished that he could have been there to listen to the kind words people spoke of her.

Misty's father along with the rest of her extended family must be well aware now that he is indeed innocent. John hopes there will be someone around to help him get to Chloe's house. The streets are empty for the first time in days. John steps down off the porch and slowly limps to the store. His body aches and his head is still a little fuzzy, yet he's determined to make it to his brother's aid.

John is relieved to find the Store owner's wife and Mr. Victor both standing together at the counter. They jump at the sound of the door, very much on edge, and gasp at the site of him. Mr. Victor rushes over to John and grabs his arm to help steady him.

"You have to sit down," he tells him.

"No," he insists quietly through a raspy voice. "I have to get to my brother, can you help me?"

"Yes, yes of course," he answers hesitantly, and then hooks a thumb to point out the side window. "I was just waiting for Leroy to grab a couple of guns and dogs from his house. We're taking him to check things out at your friends place."

Leroy Crawl is Misty's cousin. They were all together after the funeral and heard Sheriff Black explain everything that was going on. He's one of the few bear hunters around who use dogs, and was away when she went missing. John is relieved to hear he'll be around tonight to help. John has cut hay and branded cows with Leroy on several occasions, he knows him fairly well. It only takes a few minutes before Leroy, Mr. Victor and John are driving down the road to the Mead place.

CHAPTER FOURTEEN

C hloe sits in the silence of the woods, tied to a tree. She hasn't
seen Deputy Evan for the last hour. The darkening sky brings
the cold with it. She's wearing nothing except Michael's tee shirt and
she's freezing. She's frightened and every inch of her is shivering. She
searches the trees, waiting anxiously for the return of her attacker
while she recalls the events of the last horrifying hours of her life.

Earlier that evening

Chloe looks over helplessly at Michael as he sits hunched over, with
his hands tied to his ankles. In front of her is a brutal killer with a big
black duffel bag of 'tools', as he likes to call them. He pulls out one
tool at a time and forces Chloe to inspect each one. He explains
beforehand every knife, saw, and piece of wire. Rosa trembles in a
pool of her own blood clinging onto what last bit of life is left in her.

Evan pulls Rosa's head down forward and starts sawing at the
back of her neck first. She's still alive as the blade gnaws away at her
flesh and bone.

"I usually like to start with the head," he tells Chloe. "It makes their bodies more manageable. Unless I want things to last longer, like with you."

There's a slight bounce to his words, and an excitement in his eyes. He's having the time of his life. Chloe can see the inside of Rosa's neck as Evan cuts through the last of her skin. Chloe tries to close her eyes and turn her head.

"Hey," he yells. The bounce in his voice has disappeared and is replaced by a deep intimidating anger. "I told you to watch, damn girl! If you don't keep your eyes my way, then your boyfriend will be much worse off, that I can promise you."

Evan is covered in Rosa's blood, as her head falls to the floor. It rolls toward Chloe's feet and then stops in the doorway where the tile turns to carpet. The hair on the now decapitated head is matted in blood and hanging over her face. Chloe's sobs are muffled by the gag on her mouth and she struggles to take in a decent breath. She hyperventilates, and begins to numb in the fingertips.

Evan stands and admires his handy work on Rosa's body, as it hangs by the arms, headless, shooting a pulse of scarlet across the room. Chloe dry-heaves into her covered mouth trying to swallow the puke forming into her throat. Her tears are flowing. It feels like a bad dream, a nightmare that she should wake up from at any moment... but it isn't.

Michael is on the floor, fighting with his ropes. He pulls and rubs at his ankles and wrists with no luck on loosening the ties. The adrenaline of it all has made him completely oblivious to the pain he's felt in his ribs for days.

"I'm so sorry, Chloe. I'm so sorry." He cries through the struggle.

Michael can hear Evan chuckle and sneer from the bathroom as he takes his time violating and having his way with the body of Chloe's maid. Chloe looks back and forth from the gruesome scene in front of her, to Michael struggling on the floor, barely out of reach. She's losing what's left of the strength in her body, as her mind slips into a debilitating shock. Like a coping mechanism, she's shutting down in every way. After several minutes of witnessing Deputy Evan defile and dismember Rosa's body, Chloe finally gives up. She hangs her head, and lets her body slip into a state of numbness.

Chloe gives up on any hope of surviving, and her body relaxes into the confinement of her ropes. She has no fight left, not at the moment. She imagines that this disgusting man before her will soon have his way with her dead body, the same way that he is with Rosa. But there's nothing she can do about it, she's become emotionless.

Evan removes one tool at a time from his bag and cuts Rosa apart. Very last, he cuts off her toes. He explains to no one in particular, loud enough for Michael to hear every word, just how much he loves each and every toe that in that disgusting jar on Chloe's lap. In his spare time, he lays them out and tries to remember which toes belong to which girls. Its like a puzzle game for him.

Finally, Evan steps away from Rosa, and into the doorway from the bathroom to the bedroom. He's been so caught up in what he was doing with Rosa, that he'd nearly forgotten about Chloe's boyfriend, tied up against the wall. He grunts and shakes his head at the sight of Michael.

"Lucky for you Hounds boy, my plans for your girlfriend have to happen in the trees," he says with a chuckle. He tilts his head and proudly absorbs the pain in Michael's eyes. A sly smile spreads wide across his face.

"You just stay here and know that you'll never see her pretty little face again. Not the way it is now, anyway."

Michael begs and pleads for Chloe's life as Evan tosses her over his shoulder. He screams at Chloe to fight or to run and try to get away. But it's useless; Chloe has given up on her life, given up the fight. After witnessing all of the vile things he'd done with Rosa, Chloe is helpless. She only squirms and kicks for a few seconds, then limps over Evans shoulder, all of her grit drained away.

Chloe is surprised at the shape Evan is in as he packs her out of the house and into the trees. He moves quickly and efficiently, carrying both her weight, and the weight of his giant bag of tools. He's always seemed like a lazy slob of a man to her, and to everyone else around. He's now proving himself just the opposite. She wonders how many times he'd carried a body this way and how far he could go.

Chloe pays attention to Evans feet as he walks further and further into the woods. He tosses his bag and then her over deadfall before climbing it himself. He slings her back over his shoulder with ease, always keeping her at arm's length. He goes for what seems like miles, practically tireless.

After at least an hour's trek, Chloe can hear running water in front of them. There are several small streams that run through the trees, and she can't quite place their exact location. The shock is wearing off and she again begins to wonder if she has a chance of survival. She tries to memorize her surroundings as they make their way through the woods, in case escape is ever a possibility.

Chloe fears for what he'll do to her. Not only because of what she's already witnessed, but also because of the newspapers. Evan is capable of literally anything, and the unknown is paralyzing. She imagines him drowning her in one of the streams. Chloe has always loved to swim, yet still has a slight fear of the water. She hates the feeling of not being able to breathe. The suffocation, the power-lessness.

She tries to steady her breathing through the mouth gag. The smell of Evan is almost unbearable. She too is now covered in the dried blood of Rosa. It rubbed off Evan and is now all over Chloe. When he first picked her up, she could feel the warmth of Rosa's blood as it touched her bare arms and legs. It has long since dried onto both of them, in crusty chunks, everywhere except for Evans shirt. His fresh sweat has soaked his shirt from top to bottom. The scent of his perspiration alongside the rusty smell of blood is over-whelming.

Chloe is only able to breathe from her nose with the gag over her mouth. The smell stings her nostrils with every breath she draws. She wonders how far they'll go and how much longer he's physically able to carry her. Thoughts of Michael, tied up with his wrists and ankles together, yelling at her to fight, taunts her. Could she have gotten out of his clutches? Even long enough to get to her gun that was lying on her bed? Self-blame and questioning settle in.

She hadn't even thought about the gun at the time, and now it's all she can focus on. She imagines having killed Evan when she may have had the chance. She could have untied Michael and they could have gotten away together. She should have fought harder for Rosa. Tears again start to build in the corners of her eyes.

Evan approaches a stream and sets Chloe down next to the water. He keeps hold of her by a leg as he kneels down for a drink. He doesn't speak to or even look over at her. Evan puts his face directly in the running water. The stream is small, only a couple of inches deep. Chloe is grateful that the water isn't deep enough for him to force her into it.

Then he stands, takes a couple deep breaths, and hovers over Chloe for a brief moment. Knots tie themselves in her stomach, and she holds her breath, just waiting for the attack. He bends down and removes the gag from her mouth.

"You know it is useless to scream, right? We're a long way away from anyone. You can yell and beg all you want and it'll do you no good."

He smiles a mischievous grin, daring her to give it a try. She bites her lip and shakes her head in compliance. He only chuckles before bending down to pick her and his duffel bag back up off the ground.

Chloe can't believe that Evan isn't completely exhausted. It didn't take him very long to catch his breath and he's ready to continue his trek. Evan seems to be refreshed, and again excited. His pace is faster and his breathing is again steady. Evan walks up the stream, in the water for a very long way. He yells over the sound of the water for Chloe to hear.

"This is so they'll lose our tracks if anyone finds out I have you."

As they walk up a hillside, the stream shrinks to a mere drizzle. The sun is finally hiding behind the trees and there's a cool breeze biting at the backs of her bare legs. She's shivering uncontrollably now as the cold and anticipation builds up inside of her.

Evan comes into a clearing and sets Chloe down next to a lone tree, surrounded only by tall, waving grass. He plops the black bag with all of his tools right next to her. Chloe gasps, panics and starts struggling to get away. Evan smacks her across the face with the back of an opened hand.

"If you fight me, it'll only be worse," he warns. She holds back her cries as best as she can, while he ties her to the tree around her waist and arms. He grabs tightly one of her feet and reaches for a pair of wire cutters from his pack. She kicks and thrashes her body, despite his warnings.

"I said hold still!"

Chloe can't hold still, the panic is involuntary. She saw the jar of toes, and knows full well what's coming. Her top half is secured tightly to the tree, but her bottom half is going crazy. Evan keeps a tight hold of one of her legs by the ankle. He holds the sharp end of his tool around one of her toes, but it's hard to get the job done with her kicking and thrashing.

Evan is getting frustrated and impatient with Chloe fighting him. He slams the wire cutters to the ground and pulls a knife out of his bag. He pushes the blade of the knife against Chloe's throat and stares her down with his icy glare.

"If you don't hold your foot still and let me work, this knife will be the last thing you see. I'll cut out your eyes and leave you here to suffer while I go back and kill your little boyfriend before I get to you."

Chloe sucks in a deep breath, and holds it there. Her eyes are as tightly closed as she can squeeze them. Her body trembles in fear, she can't control that, but she stops kicking. *Just survive Chloe, stay alive until Michael gets loose and finds you.* Evan again grabs her foot and places her smallest toe into the wire cutters. She grinds her teeth together as hard as she can. He squeezes handles together with a *crunch*.

Chloe screams at the top of her lungs. The pain sheers through her in pulses, and her toe falls into the dirt. She forces herself to open her eyes and look at the blood pouring from the edge of her foot. She gasps, desperate for oxygen, and bites down on her lip in pain. A thick rusty taste of blood fills her mouth, from the broken meaty flesh between her teeth. After catching her breath, she squints up to see the smiling face of Deputy Evan. She pulls her knees to her chest and curls in the rest of her toes.

Evan places Chloe's toe with the others in his secret jar as a trophy.

"You know, girl, today is much different than all of the other times. I've never been this close to being caught, I have never taken more than one life in the same day, and I've never left anyone behind who knows who I am. I plan to take my time with you, and if we're found... let's just hope they kill me first."

Looking over his shoulder, knowing that he could be seen at any moment thrills him. Evan has anticipated someone walking up on him every time he's taken a girl. He's always figured that if he ever gets busted, he'll go out with a bang. Death by cop, most likely, and he'll take as many people with him to their graves as he can.

He's planned on making Chloe suffer for most of the night. Win or lose, he's ready for the outcome. If no one has found them by the morning, he'll leave this town and never look back. He'll disappear for good. Go to a new state, start over. He's angry with Sheriff Black and wants to have the last laugh, more than anything.

Chloe watches Evan closely as he builds a fire. It sparks to life, and he adds log after log, ensuring a flame that will last. It's just far enough away from her that she can feel a tiny bit of heat. Evan tells her that he doesn't want it to keep her warm, so much as light up her body and face so that he can see her pain as the hours past.

He disappears into the woods, leaving Chloe to bleed at the tree, crying for her life, and wondering about her loved ones. She sobs quietly, trying not to give him the satisfaction of seeing how much pain she's actually in. She wonders if Michael is still tied up in her room, or if anyone has found him. She thinks about Steven and his father, feeling guilty for accusing Mr. Smith. Now, she can only pray that they'll go to her house to look for her and Michael.

As Chloe sits against the tree, she remembers John and the details of his face and body being pulled behind a horse. She wonders how much time had passed since then. It's been the longest day of her life. It feels like it's been an eternity since she was reading the newspapers in Steven's basement this morning.

Chloe imagines all the things Sheriff Black must be doing to John, accusing him of murder while the real killer is just a few feet away from her, covered in Rosa's blood. The entire town knows Evan to be a disgusting and demented man. How couldn't they have put it together, she thinks?

She closes her eyes and remembers Michael's warmth, on the first night she'd slept cuddled up to him on his tiny bunk bed. It's a comforting thought. She thinks about the way his lips molded perfectly to hers in their first kiss, and the way her body reacted to his touch. Her eyes close softly, and she grins at the thought.

"What the hell is so funny?"

Evan stands over Chloe, his shadow from the fire consuming her. He stares at the peaceful look on her face, and the out of place smile on her lips. He can't imagine what in her life could be so great that she's grinning on her deathbed. Chloe's eyes shoot open at the sound of his voice. As her mind suddenly snaps back to reality, she glances around at the darkening trees and up at Evan.

"I guess we're gunna' to have to do somethin' about your new found happiness, sweetheart," he says. "Now, how do you think I should remind you of the situation that you seem to have forgotten you're in?"

He glances around in thought. Then looks down at his duffel bag, and over to the fire. His mouth curls up slightly at one side. He walks over to the fire and pulls out a branch, that's burning on one side.

"I have an idea, Honey. This is gonna' hurt."

He pulls one of her arms up and out from behind the ropes,

leaving the back of it raw and bloodied from the rub of the tree. He presses the back of his body against her face so he could get a better hold on her, securing the top of her arm in place at the base of her armpit with his side. Evan then holds the flame underneath her forearm.

The pain is unbearable. A few seconds pass and her skin is burnt to a crisp. She squeals into his body and kicks her legs uncontrollably. Evan steps away from her and watches while she swings her sore arm around in front of her and screams. He enjoys listening to her yelp in pain, especially knowing that they're far enough away for no one to hear.

Evan throws the burning branch back into the fire, and adds a couple more big logs before heaving the duffel back over his shoulder. He sets off into the thick of the trees. Chloe can't focus on or look at anything besides her burning arm. It feels as if the flames are still touching her skin. She's exhausted, and can't feel a thing outside of the crisp, pain of her forearm. It looks as if the skin has melted completely off, leaving charred meat underneath She forces herself to breathe and holds it painfully against her body.

"Please, God help me," she whispers through her sobs.

Evan emerges from the trees, and pulls one last rope out of his bag to tie her arm back to the tree. He wraps the rope around her and the tree with her arm back underneath it a few more times, and then ties it off behind her. He stands over her for several minutes enjoying his handiwork. He examines the skin hanging from her arm with pride. He even pulls in a deep breath from his nose only, taking in the scent of her burnt flesh.

"I love that smell," he grins. "I chose this place for a reason you know, look over there."

Evan crouches down next to Chloe and points into the distant trees.

She looks up, hardly able to focus her blurred sight. Through the smoke of the fire, and the cloud of her tears she strains hard to see clearly what looks like a little hut in the top of a giant oak tree. It must be where he'd disappeared to as there's a flicker of a lantern set up in the structure. It suddenly dawns on her what it is. A small tree stand sits tucked away, with a perfect line of sight. Michael and John have built a few of them over the years.

She has sat with the two, squished in a tree stand for hours on end, silently waiting for large game to come their way. They'd bet on who was the best shot, and who'd nail the prize target. John was usually the winner, he's an excellent marksman.

She now looks on to this hidden contraption in the trees with horror. Evan tells her about how he had come to the same spot years ago. He explains to her that he'd shot a victim several times with a bow, and about how Sheriff Black was there when they found her.

"This otta' bring back some fond memories for that damn fool." Evan chuckles at the thought. "You see, I even put the fire in the perfect place so you'll be lit up just right for my target practice," he snarls. Evan then bends down and breathes heavily, directly into her ear. "Don't worry, Honey. It's been a while since I shot my crossbow. I'm out of practice, so this could take all night."

Chloe is unable to speak. Her voice cuts off in her throat, hyper-ventilating from fear along with the sheer pain in her arm. Tears stream down Chloe's dirty cheeks as she watches him disappear into the darkness, anticipating the events to come.

As Chloe sits in the quiet of the night, awaiting her fate, her mind briefly drifts to the bear that she and Michael had shot a few days ago. It took hours for the creature to die, suffering, bleeding on the inside. *Once hit with an arrow or two, would it take just as long for her life to slip away*, she thinks, *would she suffer as the bear had?*

Chloe can barely make out the silhouette of him, climbing a little ladder into the tree stand. He's too far away and the smoke from the fire is blurring her view. Chloe waits helplessly for her fate. She tries with all her might to harden herself from the pain already running through her body. She watches and watches, waiting for some kind of movement from Evan. She knows that the arrows of a crossbow travel through the air fast enough that she likely won't see them coming.

She anticipates the blow of an arrow to hit her at any minute, but nothing happens, not right off. Eventually Chloe looks away from Evans direction, and down at her arm and foot. She wonders why it is taking so long for him to shoot at her, and then she realizes that it is all a part of his game. She reaches the understanding that Evan wants it to be a surprise when the arrows hit.

He wants her afraid always - the anxiety to run its course and then hit suddenly with full force when it is least expected. He's a sick man and has been playing his disgusting games with an incomprehensible number of women for years.

"Please God, please let someone find me," she begs.

CHAPTER FIFTEEN

Michael has a surge of hope that Chloe can be saved. It has been close to an hour since he watched Evan carry her off. Together, with Steven and Mr. Smith they have a much better chance of catching up to them. He hopes Evan wouldn't have been able to travel very far or very fast carrying Chloe over his shoulder. As long as she's still alive now, he'll get to her. They have a chance, if they're smart. If they're fast.

Little do they know, Sheriff Black had come up on the scene only minutes after they left. He's already let John go, and is on his way with a small posse. Close, they're very close behind. And, not too far behind them is Leroy with John and a few tracking dogs. It's all coming to a head, a race against time... against Evan.

At first, Michael, Robert and Steven fan out into the trees, walking back and forth, weaving in and out of each other's paths looking for Evans tracks. It didn't take long before Steven spotted his foot prints. They left a distinct track in the mud. It was a track that Mr. Smith recognized instantly. Mr. Smith had been the first to see these exact same footprints with Chloe when they followed his trail to Misty's torn dress and blood on the ground.

This time around it is a bit harder to follow Evan's footprints. They disappear easily in the leaves and dead fall. There's also no blood trail, less to follow. Darkness is creeping in, complicating the task even more.

The three of them hurry as fast as possible, deeper and deeper into the woods. The visible footprints are few and far between. They're losing more daylight with each step taken. They move in silence as fast as they can, trying not to lose hope. They only speak when a new footprint is found, working together to make it in the right direction. After about an hour's walk, the sun is completely behind the trees and they are unable to see any more footprints.

As the task grows harder, and the feeling of defeat creeps through Michael's bones, a faint sound of barking dogs bounces through the air. The sound is music to his ears, and a fresh surge of hope comes with it.

"Someone else must be searching!" Steven shouts.

The sound of the barking dogs moves closer and closer. There's no mistaking the direction they're moving in. Michael breathes a sigh of relief, wondering who it is, and why hadn't they used the dogs to look for Misty. He shakes off the question, it doesn't matter now. All that matters right now, at this very moment, is finding Chloe before it is too late. *Please Chloe, please still be alive*, he thinks.

"We should stay right here, and wait for the dogs." Robert says.

"No," Michael insists. "They're coming up fast, we have to keep moving. We have to get to her, one way or another. They'll catch us."

As Michael talks to Robert, he realizes that he hadn't given that morning's events another thought. Not now that the killer's identity is revealed. The look on Robert's face tells him that it's still very personal. There's a reason Robert is involved, only it isn't what they thought. Not at all. *Why did he have all of those newspapers?* Nothing makes sense to him any longer.

"Why did you come with Steven to find me and Chloe?" He asks Mr. Smith as they walk, searching the ground for another print. "I don't understand what you were doing with all that stuff... and the newspapers?"

As the barking continues to grow closer, Steven and his father fill Michael in on the events of the entire day. Robert tells Michael about his sister and his intentions for her killer. They tell him about Evan's house and all of his sketches covering the walls and the floor. Steven also tells Michael about his mom's condition now, and about how worried she was when they stopped to look for him and Chloe.

The dogs are nearing them, and they're grateful for the help. As the barking gets closer and closer, they can hear the sounds of voices along with the animals. Michael recognizes Mr. Victor instantly. He lets out a long sigh of relief as he hears John talking to him. *Oh my God, he's free,* Michael thinks. His heart skips a beat in his chest.

The dogs come into view first. There are two large red bone hound dogs with lots of extra skin around their necks, and floppy ears. Leroy is holding his animals on a very short leash, trying to keep up and veer them around the deadfall as they pull him into view. Mr. Victor and John aren't too far behind them.

Michael and Steven run straight to John's side. Mr. Victor has been helping John stay on his feet and move quickly. It hasn't been an easy task, not by a long shot, but they're determined. Assisted by adrenaline and pure heart, John is running on fumes, ready to tip over at any moment. His entire body aches and his head is light. Mr. Victor has an arm around John's waist and is carrying much of his weight while they follow the noses of Leroy's dogs further and further into the woods.

Michael immediately takes Mr. Victor's place at his brother's side, happy to assume the burden onto his own shoulders. They're each grateful to see one another alive, yet determined to keep moving. No time for the luxury of reminiscing, not tonight. Not after everything they've seen and been through, and especially not with Chloe in the clutches of the worst kind of evil. The dogs continue to sniff the ground and howl, following Evan and Chloe's trail.

Leroy shouts at them over the noise of his barking dogs.

"Deputy Evan left a shirt in the jailhouse. We took that and some clothes of your girlfriend's from her house for the dogs to sniff. They know the scent, as long as they stay on it, we'll find 'um."

Robert speeds right to Leroy's side, following the dogs as closely as possible. Steven and Michael struggle to keep John upright and moving. Mr. Victor is relieved that John has more help. He's been tiring and having a hard time keeping up himself.

Mr. Victor shouts. "These dogs sure would've come in handy when we were looking for Misty. Leroy was out of town. He just got home today, thank God."

"I just hope we're not too late," Michael replies.

"Where is Sheriff Black now?" Steven asks.

"I don't know," answers Mr. Victor. "They let John go and took off on their horses about a half an hour before we left town ourselves. They're probably miles in the wrong direction by now, I'm sure. They should've heard the dogs or met up with us by now."

Michael shakes his head in disappointment. He's not exactly surprised. Sheriff Black isn't a smart man. He had a hard-enough time finding Misty in the daylight with a massive blood trail to follow. Michael and John have both come to learn firsthand Sheriff Black's mistakes. Michael looks over at John's face and head, as he helps him walk and move. It's hard to tell the severity of his brother's wounds in the dark.

"I'm okay," John says, as he notices the concern on Michael's face.

"Of course you'd say that, John. You're so damn stubborn sometimes. What the hell are you doing out here anyway? You should've stayed in town."

"When our jackass of a Sheriff said he found another body in Chloe's house I had to make sure that you were okay," He winces and tries to quicken his stride. "Especially when he said that the house was empty and Chloe's car was there."

On the one hand Michael is upset at his brother's tenacity, but on the other hand he completely understands. Either way, it is what it is, and John is only slowing them down. He tries to convince John to stay behind now. At first, he asks his brother nicely, coming from a compassionate angle. He tries telling John to build a fire and let them take care of Chloe... of course John refuses.

They approach a small stream. Both of the dogs stop barking and sniff around for some time. They seem to have lost the scent.

"Shit!" yells Leroy.

He lets the dogs off the leash so that they can run up and down the stream.

"They're going to have to find the trail all over again. That bastard must be smarter than I gave him credit for."

Michael looks up at the forming stars in the sky. He wonders how late it is and how far Evan could've possibly taken Chloe. All of the horrible things that Evan did to Rosa are front and center in thought. He's panicked with worry for Chloe. If the dogs can't pick up their trail again, then she could be lost forever. He fights back the tears, as they again build up behind his eyes.

John puts his arm back around his brother, "We'll find her."

No sooner than the words come out, Leroy bushes past the two with an arm load of kindling to start a fire.

"Not with you we won't," he says.

"He's right," Robert jumps in. "Them dogs ain't on no leash no more. Once they find a scent, they'll take off. So, we'll have to run for it."

"But..." John starts.

"You're too slow," Leroy confirms. "You have to stay here if we have any chance of catching 'em in time. Who knows what'll happen once that Deputy hears the dogs coming."

Michael cringes at their words, and then rushes to Leroy's side to help get the fire going. Steven and Mr. Victor scramble through the closest trees to break away dead branches, and gather fallen wood. They make a small pile. The dogs splash and slosh around in the wood and mud, running up and down the banks edge on both sides.

Michael struggles to look John in the eye as the fire springs to life. It lights their faces just enough to make out detailed expressions in blanket of the night's darkness. Michael is too ashamed to look at his brother, and too ashamed to talk. He drops his chin to his chest and shakes his head. Guilt for letting Chloe slip away from his grasp nearly consumes him, like it's his fault that Chloe was taken.

The wind has picked up and he's shivering in the cold himself. Wisps of fog escapes his lips with every breath, and he can only imagine how cold Chloe has to be, if she is even still alive. He imagines her frozen, wearing nothing but his tee-shirt.

Michael passes John the pistol they'd taken from Chloe's father. The sound of the dogs howling yet again makes his heart leap into his throat. Their heads all snap in the direction of the animals. *Thank God*, Michael thinks.

"Let's go, boys!" Leroy shouts and takes off as fast as he can on foot.

He follows the sound of howls, with Robert close in tow.

Michael pulls John into a hug, wrapping his arms around his shoulders tightly. John pulls away first and gives him one short nod.

"Go," John says. "I promise I'll be right here waiting once you find her."

To Leroy, it feels much like every other time he's taken his dogs out at night racoon hunting. He's good at running through the trees. The dark offers a challenge, but it's doable nonetheless. Robert and Mr. Victor struggle to keep up, tripping up behind him along the way.

Michael grips an arm tightly around the pain in his rib as his feet move as fast as he can push them. With Steven by his side they gain ground, rushing through the dark toward the terrifying unknown.

Faintly, the smell of smoke from a campfire reaches them. The barking from the dogs ceases and they stop moving forward. The only sounds are coming from one single place. They've reached what they're after, and the men force themselves to pick up the pace to catch up. Michael knows they're close and his heart pounds, nearly out of his chest. His lungs are burning, and his eyes stinging. He's out of breath, and the pain in his ribs shoots through his core like lightning.

As they're just about up to the dogs, Robert Smith puts a hand on his gun while he runs. Evan will surely put up a fight. Even if he's unable to return the pain Evan has caused so many, at least he may have a chance to stop this monster from hurting anyone else ever again. No matter the outcome, Robert is as ready as he's ever been, as ready as he'll ever be.

The sound of a gunshot ripples through the air, and the barking of the dogs stops instantly. All five of the men halt in their tracks. Leroy listens closely for barks, but can now only hear the low, sad howls of one. The gunshot sounded way too close for comfort.

"That sun of a bitch shot my dog!" Leroy says.

The smell of smoke is strong. They continue walking... slower, quieter, trying to sneak in toward the fire. The shrill sound of Leroy's second dog yips and yelps out in pain. The trees soon come to an abrupt stop, a nearly perfect line edges a grass clearing.

Leroy crouches down, he's the first to reach the long tree line. He's hidden in the dark behind a large shrub. He tightens his jaw and clenches a fist as he looks on to see one of his pets, dead on the ground lying next to a half-naked girl.

Chloe is in perfect sight. She's covered in blood, tied up to a tree. Her face is leaning on her pulled up knees, and pointing toward him. She isn't moving and he can't tell if she's dead or alive. Leroy's second dog is running around in circles with a small arrow stuck out of his leg. Mr. Smith soon reaches the tree line right behind him, and crouches down next to a tree close by.

"He is in the trees," Leroy says. "waiting to shoot us just like he did my dogs. We have to find him before we untie her. It looks like she might already be dead."

Just as the words come out, Chloe lifts her head, and in a shrill voice she screams.

"Help me!"

CHAPTER SIXTEEN

C hloe can hear a faint sound of dogs in the distance. A rush of relief and adrenalin streams through her. She bends her legs up tightly to her body and sets her forehead on her knees.

"Please God, let them be coming for me. Please don't let them get hurt."

She begs and pleads in quiet prayer as the sound of the animals grows closer. The tears stream down her face, thick and salty. This is when the first arrow is finally slung in her direction. She hears it flying through the air for just a brief moment before it hits. *Whishew,* followed by a small *thud* as it sticks in the ground below her body. It misses her already wounded foot by just a couple inches, and sticks into the blood-stained ground. Chloe's heart races as she stares at the arrow in front of her.

She wonders if Evan heard the dogs as well, and if he's going to kill her fast before help can reach her. Will he continue to torture her with the arrows and let her die a slow and painful death; or just get it all over with and shoot her with the rifle? She continues to pray and wait, as the sound of the barking dogs approaches. There's another quiet whistle in the air as the sound of the second arrow is being flung in her direction. She holds her breath, preparing herself for the impact. It grazes the side of her shoulder and sticks into the tree.

The sting of its slice is fast and sharp. The trickle of blood runs down her arm and soaks the rope that has her restrained against the tree. The pain of Chloe's burnt arm is still so much stronger than the new, fresh wound. She shakes against the bark of the tree, helpless and afraid. Her breath is shallow, and she tries to focus on the sound of the dogs approaching, clinging to the hope of a continued life.

The reality that a bullet or arrow could claim her life at any moment is intense, too real and too incomprehensible to fully take in. She waits and waits but nothing else comes, not right away. It seems like a lifetime of catching her breath through the sobs, time slows down, the woods are still.

The barking of dogs grows louder, and soon she watches them emerge from the tree line one at a time and into the clearing. They race towards her howling, and sniffing the dirt all around. The first dog to come into site gains ground. Just as he's a few feet away, there's a loud *Bang*. It echoes in the trees, and he drops lifelessly to the ground. Chloe watches as the second dog lets out a couple of long shallow barks before slowly approaching his companion. He circles around his partner, whimpering and occasionally nudging him with his nose.

He approaches Chloe, plants a giant wet lick up the length of her face, and then returns to his friend who lies lifelessly on the ground next to her. Chloe watches the dogs and wonders how far behind them the owners could be. Would Evan kill them the same way he's killed their dogs? Is Michael with them? Chloe's heart bleeds for the lifeless animal, and the image of Rosa's headless body crosses her mind. Chloe shuts her eyes tightly waiting for Evan to make his next move.

The next arrow shoots through the air and sticks in the back leg of the whimpering dog. He yips and takes off, hopping around in circles on his other three feet. Chloe's lips and fingers are numb and her shaking is uncontrollable. She hears a faint voice coming from the trees. It is quiet, she can't make out who it belongs too, so she takes her chance and shouts at the top of her lungs.

"Help me!"

Just as she yells, Michael darts past the sound of muffled voices.

"Stop," a man yells from behind him. "You'll be shot Michael, wait!"

Michael doesn't listen, he can't. Steven is right behind him. Emerging from the trees, only to be stopped by Mr. Smith. Another gunshot rings through the air. Evan's bullet zooms past Michael's ear, close enough to be heard. Michael drops to the ground next to her. As fast as he can, he pulls a knife from his pocket and begins sawing through her restraints.

"I'm gunna' get you out of here," he promises, as another arrow thuds into the tree above their heads.

Chloe's body convulses and shakes as the ropes loosen and fall around her. Her voice is caught in the back of her throat. She tries to focus her eyes into the tree stand over the dying fire as Michael hurries to free her. The smoke is thick and the light of the fire is dimming. Another arrow flings past them, this time missing the tree completely.

Leroy shouts to his dog from the tree line. Chloe watches it limp off to him as Michael hooks an arm around her waist to help her up. Chloe doesn't recognize the voice but catches a glimpse of Leroy as well as Steven along the tree line. They're out of sight from the tree stand. She breathes a sigh of relief, as Michael scoops her up into his arms. Chloe strains to see Evan's post through the darkness and smoke of the fire. She's able to make out the silhouette of him, climbing down the ladder and onto the ground.

"He's coming," she whispers and buries her face into the crook of his shoulder.

"What do you mean? From Where?" Michael asks.

He searches all around them into the woods, trying to see any sign of Evan himself. She points a weak finger in Evans direction as he disappears completely out of sight into the trees. As soon as

Michael reaches the tree line, he sets Chloe on her feet and holds onto her tightly around the waist with one arm. He thumbs the tears from her face and stares down at her. Only moments ago, he feared she was dead, and now here she is. Standing before him, breathing, and in one bloody piece.

"He's going to kill you," she whispers.

Michael doesn't respond to her comment, he just squeezes her icy body tightly against his. He breathes in the scent of her, feels the rise and fall of her chest. Leroy rips off his jacket and wraps it around her in their embrace. Then he pats his wounded dog on the top of his head, clicks a bullet into the chamber of his rifle, and searches around into the darkened trees.

"Where did you see him last?" Mr. Smith demands.

"He was that way," Chloe points a trembling finger. "Climbing out of a tree."

"Get her to John's fire, son," Mr. Victor says. "We'll take care of this ass hole."

The sound of Mr. Victors voice startles Chloe. She hadn't seen him walk up on them. She's lost, confused, and afraid. She can't quite place where she is as her mind continues to blur.

"He's right," Steven says. "And hurry."

Everything goes blurry around her, and her knees begin to buckle. The weight of her arms feel like a ton of bricks, and the shooting pain in her foot has caused the entire bottom half of her leg to numb. Her blood loss is great, and her vision continues to blacken. Michael grabs her, scooping her body back into his arms before she falls completely to the ground. Michael locks eyes with Mr. Smith.

"You have to kill him!"

Robert nods in return, before snapping his neck in the direction of crunching twigs in the distance. Michael takes off with Chloe in the opposite direction, determined to get her away before Evan has a chance to follow. Chloe is his priority, he has to get her to safety. They need to get her warm and stop her bleeding before it's too late. Michael can't lose her again, not tonight, not ever. With the light of the nearly full moon only, he runs through the trees with her in his arms, back tracking the exact same way from which they came.

Chloe opens her eyes periodically, only to see the distraught on Michael's face, then fades back out. She does this several times. Like flashes of life. Every time she wakes, the burning pain in her arm and foot rushes through her veins causing everything to again blacken.

After a few minutes of trying to stay coherent, the sound of gunshots blasts through the air behind them. Michael clenches her body even tighter to his chest. He stands still and listens. A few more shots fire, this time they sound even further away than the first. The fear holds her wakefulness, and the tears return to her eyes in full force as she wonders who exactly is doing the shooting, and who may be on the receiving end.

"It's all my fault," she cries.

"Don't say that," he whispers and kisses her on the forehead. "Hang on tight, we have to keep moving."

The adrenaline moves Michael at an unbelievable pace. Every time a new gunshot fires, he moves a little quicker. It doesn't take long for them to reach John at his fire by the small stream. He's built up the flames to an impressive height. He's sitting on the ground a little way away, absorbing the heat with his head in his hands. Chloe is still incredibly light headed, but she wants to stand. Just for a moment, she needs to find her own strength. Michael sets her on her feet by the fire, but keeps his arm around her waist for support.

The warmth of the fire is lifesaving. She shivers in Michael's arms, leaning into him. Still fuzzy, still confused. John rushes to them.

"Oh my God," he says, "Chloe, you're alive!"

She's unable to form words, and her knees again weaken.

"Quick," Michael tells him, "we have to get her warm and cleaned up."

Michael sits on the dirt by the fire, pulls her onto his lap, and scoops her legs up into Leroy's coat. John takes off his shirt and rips it into several strips. He dips the torn pieces into the stream one after another and hands the wet cloths to Michael.

Together they clean the blood from her skin and inspected her wounds. The tip of Chloe's foot is still streaming blood from the empty space of a missing toe. Michael tightens his belt around her ankle to slow the flow. They wrap her entire foot, and John puts pressure on the wound. Chloe screams out in pain, and grits her teeth. Again, she buries her face into Michael's chest and sobs.

The gash on her shoulder from an arrow also cut deep into her flesh. It sliced all the way across, exposing the meat. She's still losing an unbelievable amount of blood from the open gash. Michael cleans around it as best as he can and then wraps a strip of John's shirt underneath her armpit and around the wound. The pain from all the pressure again causes Chloe to lose consciousness.

They don't even know where to start with the burned flesh from her elbow to wrist. It's charred through layers. There's hardly any skin left on a large portion of her arm. They don't want to smother it, or let anything touch it for fear of infection. They decide to leave it be, for now until they have help.

"I wish we were closer to mom," John says. "She'd know what to do."

"Me too," Michael agrees. "Steven said she was doing awful."

"Shit. I hope she's okay."

Chloe slips in and out of wakefulness. She leans back against Michael and feels his heartbeat against her back. She takes in the warmth of his cheek against hers. They're positioned with her burned arm away from the heat of the fire. The cold wind feels refreshing against it, as the rest of her body is finally warming.

Michael tightens his arms around her waist and breathes in her scent. He gently kisses the base of her neck and pulls her tighter against himself. He wishes he could take her place and absorb all her pain. He thanks God that she's safe in his arms, though a nagging guilt tells him that because she's away and safe with John, that he needs to go back.

"I love you," he whispers in her ear.

Chloe closes her eyes and lets herself feel the depth of his words. It settles in her soul, consuming every inch of it.

"I love you too, Michael Hounds."

An occasional sound of gunfire reaches them from the direction they came. It echoes in the dark. Michael feels helpless, like he should be out there looking for Evan in the woods with Steven. What if he could help, what if he's supposed to be the one to put a stop to all of this?

"Maybe I should go back," he mumbles, "I should help."

Chloe grabs his arms and shakes her head in fear. Her body tenses on his lap, and she begs.

"Please don't go! Don't leave me."

Michael tightens his grip on her, but only for a moment. He gives her a reassuring kiss on the lips. Slow. Passionate.

"Just stay right here," he tells her. "Stay with John, everything will be okay."

"Please, Michael."

"Chloe, I can't just sit here and let him get away. I love you. I promise I'll come back. I'll always come for you."

He slips out of her grip, helping situate her against John's side. Nuzzled carefully in the crook of John's arm. Before he can leave the warmth of the fire the sound of an animal's footsteps and a voice comes from the trees just a few feet away from them. John draws his pistol and points it steadily in the direction of the noise. He's ready, whatever comes out of the tree's he's ready to protect Chloe and himself at all cost.

"Don't shoot!"

Sheriff Black comes into view, along with the same lawmen and Trudge brothers from earlier.

"We heard a couple of hound dogs a while back, and gunshots too. We followed the sounds and the smell of smoke here." The Sheriff says.

He doesn't look any further than John as he jumps off Ol' Blue and ties him to a tree. When he walks further into the light he real-izes that it is Chloe, propped up against John... bloodied and bandaged. He's shocked at the sight of her, and runs to her side, followed by both of the Trudges.

"Are you okay?" one asks.

"What happened?" questions the other.

Chloe can't speak, she only sobs, and shakes her head. The Sheriff sighs, and reaches for her hand. The bigger of the lawmen adjusts his belt as usual, and mumbles to himself in a low somber voice.

"What did he do to you?"

"You're a little late don't you think?" Michael demands, with his fists balled at his sides.

"Where are they?" The Sheriff asks, ignoring Michael's attitude. If anyone has earned the right to be upset, it's Michael Hounds, the Sheriff thinks. "Where's Evan and your friends?"

"That way!" Michael exclaims hooking a thumb in the direction of the occasional gunshots. "I'm going back. Steven, his dad, Leroy Crawl, and Mr. Victor are all out there where we found Chloe. We keep hearing gunshots. We need to hurry."

CHAPTER SEVENTEEN

S teven darts through the darkened wilderness, jumping over bushes and ducking branches as he goes. It's hard to move fast in the thickness of the woods. Another gunshot whizzes past his ear, but he keeps running. He's lost his dad, and Evan has been a step ahead of them. Trying his damndest to get a good shot in the dark, mostly at Steven.

Steven kneels down behind a bush to catch his breath. Steven realizes that he needs to make some kind of a game plan if he has any hope of survival. *What the hell am I doing*, he asks himself? He thinks about how he'd peed his pants only a few hours ago. Now he's running like a madman, no plan, no focus. *It's no wonder he's after me more than the others*, Steven realizes. He hopes that they're at least circling and moving in on Evan as he acts as bait or a distraction for them.

Steven convinces himself to focus, to think like a predator rather than prey. He can smell the smoldering smoke from the fire that was by Chloe. The light projected by the moon is limited. He can see a few yards into the trees around him in every direction but other than that, it's all blackness. He pulls back the hammer on his pistol and makes a conscious effort to steady his hands.

Steven begins to move slowly in the shadows of the trees and bushes as quietly as he possibly can. If he can't see then neither can Evan. He silently moves back toward the tree line. He stays low and weaves his way between the tallest bushes. Soon he's hidden in the shadow of a giant tree with branches hanging over his head. The leaves and shrubs of the brush around it engulf him. He's hidden completely from sight, unless he moves. It's a waiting game now, and hopefully Evan will cross his sights.

Steven strains his ears until he can make out a nearby sound. It's a soft liquid filled, whispering cry for help. His heart leaps in his chest, as he assesses the situation. He has to force himself not to run to the noise. Steven thinks about all the times he's used dying rabbits as bait to call in coyotes. Evan could easily be using the same tactic. Steven inches his way around the trunk of the tree, and slowly peaks his head around the brush.

Mr. Victor is on the ground, in a pool of scarlet liquid.

"Please," he cries, clinging to life. "Someone. Help."

His voice is raspy, full of fluid. Steven can barely decipher the words as they spurt and sputter from his dying mouth. Blood pours from the corner his lips, and his body begins to twitch. He's been shot twice... once in the neck, and once in the lower stomach. He lies there with his hands clenched around his neck, blood squirting in all directions. After a few more coughs and pleads, Mr. Victor's hands fall to the ground and his head rolls to the side. His body continues to twitch for a few seconds, and finally goes still.

Steven feels helpless. He continues to fight back the urge to run to Mr. Victor's side. A tear trickles down his face as he sits in the brush, waiting for movement in the trees around Mr. Victor's dead body. *This is it, you pig,* he thinks, *you have to come out now.* Steven holds his gun tightly, waiting for Evan to approach his latest victim. Based on Evan's return to Misty's remains, Steven assumes Evan won't be able to help himself. He'll want a close-up look at his latest victim.

He assumed correctly. Evan soon creeps silently out of the trees. Steven moves as slowly as possible, so as to not make any noise. He positions his gun in front of his eyes, and lines up his sights directly at Evan's heart. He slides his finger over the trigger and gives it a squeeze.

The gun fires and Evan jumps. The bullet grazes past his body, and hits a tree behind him. Just as fast, Evan lifts his rifle to his shoulder to shoot back at Steven. Before he has a chance to aim, another man darts out of the bushes and pounces on top of him. Evan's gun fires into the air. It's Leroy, and he's grabbed Evan's arm in attempt take the rifle. Leroy has been hiding close by, just the same as Steven. Dirt flies as they roll around on the ground. Steven hurries to the ruckus of them wrestling around. There's a rustle in the trees next to them, and some snapping of branches. Steven squints to see his father running in their direction.

"No, Steven!" Robert yells as he runs.

Steven is standing directly between his approaching father and the fighting Leroy and Evan. The rifle again fires from the moving clump of grown men in a cloud of dust on the ground. The bullet hits Leroy dead center in the chest, firing straight through his heart. The exit comes out clean, right between his shoulder bones, shooting a trail of blood into the air.

Evan pushes Leroy's heavy body off himself with a swift heave. He jumps up and puts his last bullet in the chamber. He's fast and focused. Robert is now only a couple of yards away, running toward him full speed ahead. Steven looks back and forth between the two. With a sudden panic he jumps. Steven dives into the gap of air between his running father and the barrel of Evan's rifle.

The shot fires. Impact of the shot sends Steven's body in the opposite direction. The bullet connected, shooting directly through the middle of him. He hits the ground with a hard *thud,* and slides across the dirt. Robert leaps over Steven's body as it hits the ground. He too lunges onto Evan. Both his and Evans' guns are out of bullets.

Robert has the upper hand, he's stronger and passionate. He slams Evan's head into a rock on the ground knocking him unconscious instantly. As the tears roll down his face Robert slams the butt of his pistol into Evan's face, again and again. Blood gushes out from his nose and mouth, but Robert can't stop. Several blows later, Evan is within an inch of his life. Robert stands, his knees weak. He wipes the blood, snot and tears from his face, and rushes to his dying son.

Steven gasps for air. He tries to focus his increasingly blurred vision onto is blood-soaked father.

"I'm sorry, dad."

It's the only words he can manage to spit out as the last breath escapes from his chest.

"No!" Robert cries.

Robert wraps himself around his son's limp body and lifts him onto his lap.

"Please, no."

Robert rocks back and forth, holding Steven in his shaking arms. He sits there with Steven on his lap for what seems like forever, sobbing and unable to move. Steven's face is blank and lifeless. It's growing lighter in color, with a streak of blood from his mouth.

Evan begins to stir. He rolls to his side, and coughs up blood. Robert gently sets Steven's body aside, and stomps over to Evan. He flops Evan over onto his stomach, and hits him again with the back of his gun. The blow knocks him unconscious. Robert grabs Evan by the ankles, and with all the strength he can muster, begins to pull Evan's body. Inch by inch he pulls the limp body into the same clearing where he had Chloe tied to the tree. Evan is a round and heavy man. They're almost to the base the tree when Michael and Sheriff Black run up, followed by their small herd of men.

Michael gasps at the sight of Steven's dead body, and falls to his knees at his friend's side. He stares at Steven's still bleeding body and the pool of red liquid all around him. Michael then looks up at

Robert, pulling Evan by the feet. He knows what's coming, where Robert is taking him. They all do. Michael runs to his aid before anyone has a chance to interject. Robert's face is covered in streaks of blood and tears, and he's sweating profusely. Michael grabs one of Evan's feet, relieving Mr. Smith of half the weight.

The Sheriff looks around at the bloodbath before him. Mr. Victor, Leroy, and Steven all lay dead in the cool of the night. They were all shot dead within just a few yards of each other. The Sheriff then looks over at and Robert and Michael dragging Evan through the dirt and shrubs. The other two lawmen are panting and gasping for air. They'd left their horses back with John and Chloe. They're out of shape and hardly able to keep up.

"We have to get him back for a trial before they kill him," says the belt adjuster.

"No," insists the Sheriff with a stern commanding voice. "We'll help them hang him."

The Sheriff recalls the last time he was in this exact place. He remembers every detail of the dead girl that had been tied up and shot at from a distance, from what they believed at the time to be a crossbow. *Of course, Evan would bring her here*, thinks the Sheriff as he shuffles to the tree and places a finger on one of the arrows now stuck in it. He shakes his head in frustration. He's angry at Evan and he's disappointed him himself for not thinking of this spot in the first place.

The Trudge men are already busy tying a rope and testing the branches of the tree, as Michael and Robert drop Evan's legs to the dirt. The two lawmen slowly approach the contemplating Sheriff. The smaller of the two shakes his head, he's baffled by it all.

"Are you sure you want to do this?" he asks, already knowing the answer.

"Yes."

"I actually agree," adds the larger of the two. "I've never seen anything like this bastard. He deserves to hang. What better place for him to die than here?"

Wordless, without the need of discussion, everyone is ready. Sheriff Black looks around at his colleagues, staring at the blood-soaked serial killer at their feet. He gives the dangling end of the rope to Mr. Smith. They lock eyes for a brief moment, and Robert gives him a nod, without exchanging a single word.

Mr. Smith, still in silence, wraps the loop of the rope around Evan's neck. Just as they all grab hold of the end to pull Evan off the ground by his neck, Mr. Smith finally finds his voice.

"Wait!" he shouts, covered in the blood of his son with a burning stare in his eyes. "I want him to be awake when we hang him. I want to see the look on his face as he dies."

The men comply without complaint. Though he'd never say it out loud, Sheriff Black feels the same. He too wants to see Evan suffer. He wants Evan conscious and aware of his own death, to know how it felt so see his life coming to an end. It isn't fair to any of the families of his victims, it isn't proper justice otherwise. Not a word is spoken in protest. They stand still, waiting for Evan to come to. Each of them with the rope in hand, single file behind Robert Smith, they're ready to play their part in his death.

After a few minutes Evan slowly wakes. At first, he's dumbfounded and confused. Evan locks eyes with Robert, and then Michael. The connection is made fast, and he struggles to his feet with the aid of the tree. Hunched at the middle, he reaches up and feels the rope around his neck. He takes a step to run, and Robert Smith is the first to jerk on the rope.

The notion is followed by all the rest of the men in unison. They pull the rope with all their strength and walk backwards, heaving one step at a time. Evan slowly lifts off the ground by his neck. His legs are kicking and he grabs at the rope with his hands, pawing viciously. He gasps for air and jerks his body around for a full minute before his body goes limp... lifeless. His bodily fluids trickle into the dirt under his feet. All seven men holding the rope stay still. They hold their ground and the rope until they're completely certain that there isn't an ounce of life left.

"It's done," says the Sheriff.

The men let go of the rope and Evan's dead body falls to the ground in a heap. They all stand around him speechless. One of the Trudge men nudges Evan's foot with his own. This isn't how any of them imagined things playing out.

"What the hell are we supposed to do now?" Michael asks.

Mr. Smith hangs his head, as he turns back to tend to his dead son. Michael nods to himself, agreeing silently to let the rest of the men deal with the mess. He has to help with Steven and he has to get back to Chloe. Nothing else matters anymore, it's done, Evan is dead. Robert scoops Steven's body into his arms and starts walking.

Together they walk in the dark. Steven will be put to rest, and Chloe will live. Michael has hope that maybe someday peace can be found in their hearts again. The events of the last few days will shape and change them all forever.

ABOUT THE BOOK

Sketch is a rendition of The Stix, by Didi Oviatt.
The Stix was published by America Star Books in 2013. It is now
and forever forward, out of print. The Stix was the first book written
by Didi Oviatt. If you're lucky enough to get your hands on a
paperback copy then hang onto it, as there were less than one
hundred ever printed. Sketch is a completely flipped, re-written, and
improved upon version of The Stix.

ABOUT THE AUTHOR

Didi Oviatt is an intuitive soul. She's a wife and mother first, with one son and one daughter. Her thirst to write was developed at an early age, and she never looked back. After digging down deep and getting in touch with her literary self, she's writing mystery/thrillers like *Search For Maylee, Justice for Belle, Aggravated Momentum, The Stix, New Age Lamians (a trilogy to be), and more,* along with a six-piece short story collection called the *Time Wasters.* She's also collaborated with Kim Knight in an ongoing interactive short story anthology *The Suspenseful Collection.* When Didi doesn't have her nose buried in a book, she can be found enjoying a laid-back outdoorsy lifestyle. Time spent sleeping under the stars, hiking, fishing, and ATVing the back roads of beautiful mountain trails, and sunbathing in the desert heat play an important part of her day to day lifestyle.

Following is the first chapter of Search For Maylee. Enjoy!

SEARCH FOR MAYLEE
CHAPTER ONE

Autumn drew in a lungful of California air. Although it was thick, it was somehow refreshing. She looked to her side at the sun glistening off small choppy waves on the oceanfront. It sparkled in bright flashes across the horizon. She was really going to miss this stunning morning view. A thin lilac tank-top dampened with sweat in the center of her back. Her feet were growing heavy, but she pushed herself and quickened her stride. Autumn had been running along the beach every day, sometimes a few times a day, for the past three years. She found that running helped to clear her mind, and tiring her body helped her sleep at night.

Every day, during this run, the thought of Maylee's disappearance raced through Autumn's mind on a loop. Every intricate detail was recalled, in order, exactly as it happened. She remembered what Maylee had eaten for breakfast, and dropping her off at school that morning. Even the conversation they had still haunted her:

"Don't you want some eggs?" Maylee chirped in her perky morning voice.

"Nah, I'll just grab a coffee."

"Whatever Aunt Autumn, you're going to sneak one of those

disgusting greasy processed breakfast muffins after you drop me off, aren't you?"

Accusing eyes pierced Autumn's embarrassed face, forcing her to blush. Strange, how such a young woman could find so much fault over an innocent guilty pleasure, no bigger than a thin slice of cheese with sausage.

These memories continuously floated in and out of Autumn's mind, circling her like a consuming shadow, just waiting for the right moment to swallow her whole. After reliving the worst day of her life, Autumn would clear her mind, steady her breath, and convince herself to focus on the present. It felt like an impossible task to stop living in the past. Maylee was Autumn's niece, and she was seventeen years old when she was taken. Maylee was a high school senior with two weeks left until her graduation. She had her entire life ahead of her.

Now, three years later, Autumn was convinced that if she could just remember any tiny detail, something she may have skipped over, the police would be forced to pry Maylee's case back open. Autumn was more of a mother to Maylee than her junkie sister could ever dream of being -- even on a sober day.

It had been nearly an hour since today's run commenced. Time seemed to escape Autumn as the worn-out sneakers laced to her feet moved further down the beach. Her legs were starting to tingle and burn. They weakened and felt like noodles under her wearying body. The intake of air burned her chest, leaving her throat to feel like a charred tree -- still intact and alive, but with the edges burnt to a crisp. She could feel the color of her face darken as fresh oxygenated blood sped through her veins.

Over the course of the last few days, she had pushed herself even further than her usual run. She would be leaving her beautiful home in Northern California, and moving to a small cramped one-bedroom apartment right in the center of Denver Colorado. Every detail of her life would change once again, and it was terrifying.

Autumn fell into a deep depression when Maylee went missing, and she became obsessed with the case. The only time she would leave the house was to go to the grocery store or police station. Her life's purpose became nothing more than to pester Detective Chance, or just Chance, as everyone called him. His full name and title were Detective Chance Rupert Lizhalia III. Clearly, the comfort of being referred to so casually by his first name was developed very early on in his career. The details and progress of Maylee's case were poked and prodded at by Autumn daily. It was a repetitive process until about five months after Maylee had disappeared. At that point, Chance put Maylee's folder on an overstuffed shelf to collect dust.

"We have done everything we can," he told Autumn on that bizarrely hot fall afternoon as he slowly wiped the sweat from his full, perfectly squared hairline.

"So you're going to throw her away? Just like that, you're done?" Autumn demanded, tears welling.

"Every police station in the country has Maylee's picture." Chance reminded her. "If anyone finds her or comes across anything that we can link to the case, then I assure you, Autumn, you'll be the first to know."

The short conversation had rendered Autumn mute. She stood frozen in shock as he told her to move on with her life. Chance apologized for the loss in such a way that it was clear -- Maylee would never be found. Then he brushed past her in the hallway of an over-lit police station, and went about his day as if nothing had changed.

Autumn recalled it now as she ran, remembering the cold emptiness in Chance's expression. The excruciating heat of that day hadn't even touched the icy daggers he sent jabbing into her chest. Even his outfit was seared into her memory. He wore a dark gray suit, complementing his tan, and an orange tie.

There was no denying it, Chance was a very attractive man for his age. The stress of the job was surely the culprit of a cluster of wrinkles at the corners of his eyes, although they only added to his enticing façade. Chance was the kind of man that you could take one look at and just know, without a doubt, he could defend himself. His build was strong enough to be noticed, with broad shoulders and a flat stomach, but his eyes were key. They were light gray and deeply piercing, always with a sharp gaze -- like an eagle ready to swoop.

The afternoon Maylee's case was practically declared unsolvable and doomed for a cold shelf life, all hope drained from Autumn. Her car was left in the parking lot, and slow, dragging feet carried her home, she moved in a blurry haze. Amidst the draining three mile walk to her front porch, the heat transformed into gloom, and before Autumn knew it, she was engulfed in rain. The weather as unforgettably odd.

The door swung open, and she collapsed onto the floor, unable to take in air. Anxiety surged through her body in waves, and salty tears streamed down her face. God only knows how long she lay paralyzed on the floor before she got up and ran out the door. Pushing herself through the stinging oversized drops of rain, she rounded a corner and made her way to the beach. Giant deadly ocean swells had never looked so inviting, but she refused stop, continuing to run faster. Step after painful step in the sand, she pushed forward.

Oxygen eventually stopped reaching her lungs, and her legs gave out. Several times Autumn collapsed to her knees and stared into the water while she wheezed and struggled for breath. Each time the *slosh* of wet sand sounded beneath her fallen body, she would pick herself back up and continue to run. By the time she returned home the sky had turned black, and there were no stars to be found. Autumn was completely surrounded by darkness, a perfect match to the way she felt inside.

A haunting recollection of her own swollen, bloodshot eyes staring back at her from the hallway mirror now left an imprint in Autumn's mind. On that traumatizing day she became a ghost – an empty shell of her once prominent self. Maylee's absence was officially real, there was a sense of finality, a permanence that made Autumn sick.

That night after her first run, the world went completely black. As soon as her head hit the pillow, exhaustion and grief took over, blocking out whatever was left of her subconscious. For the first time in those five miserable months, her body gave up. She had slept an entire night through, deep and dreamless. It was the first night without nightmares and cold sweats since Maylee went missing.

Since that painful day, Autumn continued to repeat that same beachside run. Slowly over time, she's made an effort to put her life back together. So far that effort has proven unsuccessful.

This would be the day Autumn was going to take what could possibly be the biggest step of her life. Giving up on Maylee was not an option. This move was bound to uncover something. It had to. The winding road came upon a corner and revealed a small deserted parking lot. She was close to home now, with only a few more blocks to go before the first 'For Sale' sign came into view. The signs were pointing in the direction of her striking oceanside condo.

Autumn slowed her stride to a heavy-footed jog until she reached the lawn in front of her newly sold home. No sooner than her sneakers had sunk into the freshly cut grass, she bent at the core and clutched her knees tightly, knuckles whitening, to catch her breath. Autumn glanced up to notice the front door had been opened a crack. She squinted over the top of her right shoulder, then abruptly to the left, peering down the road as far as she could see. There were no cars out of the ordinary aside from the large U-Haul sitting a few yards away.

Paranoia was common for Autumn. A constant nagging fear weighed in her chest at all times, she was forever burdened by this. It had taken a full year to convince herself to sell all of her belongings and take this giant leap. She had to be strong, and she had to leave California, for Maylee. With caution in each step, Autumn slowly made her way up to the condo. She peeked into each window, then tilted an ever-listening ear toward the crack in the door.

"Oh, for hell's sake Autumn, you're such a weirdo! You're going to pack up all of your shit and take off on some 'save the world trek', and you can't even walk into your own house without panicking!"

The voice was shrill and mocking. It belonged to Candace,

Maylee's mother. Autumn exhaled and walked inside. The sight of her sister leaning against the bar that connected the kitchen to the dining room was a lot to take in. Candace was tall and skinny. Too skinny, Autumn noted. One bony leg was crossed over the other and a thick string of smoke lifted into the air from the cigarette burning between her fingertips. She rolled her eyes at Autumn dramatically, and then flicked a long ash onto the floor.

"Candace, do you really need to do that? You know I don't let anyone smoke in my house. You think it's okay to just ash all over the place?"

"Who cares, you sold it anyway."

Candace walked over and ran what was left of her smoldering cigarette under water and dropped it into an otherwise spotless ceramic sink. The condo was empty, making it seem even bigger than usual. Autumn looked around her home, holding back the tears that were soon to inevitably flow -- it was only a matter of time. The floors transformed from a dark marbled tile to white carpet in the living room. The ceilings were vaulted and the countertops were black with marbled gray granite.

Autumn had married at a young age and lost her husband in a car accident shortly after. She had only known Keith for seventeen months total. A vow was made to herself when he died, she would never love another and that was final. It'd been eighteen years since the accident, and so far she'd stuck to her promise. Autumn went back to her maiden name, Brown, in an effort to help herself move on from the trauma of his death. Keith had come from money and left Autumn a rich young woman at the time.

Initially, she bought the condo along with a dependable used car. Then she placed what was left of the settlement into a steady monthly income that was meant to last 20 years. Since then, the car had been traded in for a newer model, an end of this cash flow was rapidly approaching, and the condo sold. Autumn was trudging unfamiliar ground as her entire life was growing foreign, and that didn't even include her job.

After the loss of her young love, the years passed and the cost of living grew. Her fixed monthly income was barely enough to pay the bills and keep her fed. Enjoying nights out with her girlfriends, or buying new outfits were rare. A few years after Keith passed, Autumn picked up a job working as a waitress in a small crab shack just down the road from her condo. Surprisingly she absolutely adored it. It didn't bring in much money, but it was enough for the little extras, and it kept her busy.

As Autumn stood across from Candace in her freshly emptied kitchen, her mind wandered to the saddened look of shock on her boss's face when she'd quit. Autumn walked away from the steady job she loved, just over a week before. Candace cleared the tar blockage from her throat, pulling Autumn back to reality.

"How did you get in here?" Autumn asked. "And did you get me that address? I'm leaving soon. I only have a few more things to pack, so I need it. You promised."

"You always leave that window in the back unlocked," Candace said with another roll of her glassed-over eyes. "And yes, I have your damn address."

Candace dug a small wrinkled piece of damp paper from her pocket, along with a chunk of dirty pocket lint and a couple of pennies. The goods were slapped onto the empty countertop. Candace then shifted restlessly on her feet, her eyes darting from one side of her head to the other. The look of a wild animal had taken over her face, as if assessing the possibility of an unexpected dash for the door. Unpredictable and permanently on edge, she finally continued in her scratchy smoker's voice.

"I still don't think you should do this. Craig's not a bad guy, he just gets a bad rep because of his record. Maylee's gone because she never paid attention to anything going on around her. It's probably her own fault she was taken, I'm sure Craig had nothing to do with it."

Aside from the obvious itch to leave, Candace was without emotion, utterly careless about Maylee. She spoke as if Maylee wasn't her daughter at all, but some strange girl she'd met on the street. It made Autumn's stomach wrench hearing her sister talk this way about her own child, her flesh and blood. How could she?

The thought of the opened back window was intentionally brushed aside. Autumn didn't even want to know exactly how her sister was privy to that information. The place would be deserted in a few hours, left for the new owners to deal with. The only thing that mattered now was how clearly strung-out and cold-blooded Candace was. A surge of anger flowed through Autumn.

Autumn couldn't stand Candace for the evil woman she'd grown into. The fact that Candace cared more about herself and getting her next fix than she did about her own daughter was sickening. Autumn stormed over to the bar and snatched up the piece of paper. It wouldn't be out of the ordinary if Candace were to change her mind, steal back the address, and make a crazy dash for the door. Frankly, it came as quite a shock to Autumn that her junkie sister had actually followed through on her promise to retrieve it in the first place. Once the address was safely in hand, Autumn finally spoke her mind.

"Maylee hated that man, and the rest of your friends. She was scared of him! She ended up here ninety percent of the time because you were a shitty mom, and your shitty friends are all terrible people. Open your eyes Candace, when are you going to understand that he was the only real lead the cops ever had? Now get the hell out of my house!"

Candace took a step back, shocked at Autumn's outburst. Her head tilted forward allowing her eyes to be shaded by the lowering of her brows. The shifty feet that struggled to hold up her stick-like legs for the first time held still. They had gotten in several fights about Maylee over the years. They brawled more since Maylee's disappearance than ever before. Candace knew she hadn't been the best mom to Maylee, but she would never admit it out loud, and she didn't much care either way. Excuses were constantly shelled out for her behavior as she never even wanted a child in the first place. Candace justified her actions to herself in any way she could.

Autumn wasn't the only one with resentment, as Candace

genuinely returned the disdain. For most of their lives Candace hated her sister for being the pretty one, the favorite. A prominent loathing of Autumn's perfection had taken up residence in Candace. There was even a slight anger toward Maylee for confiding in Autumn as much as she did. Candace would leave Maylee for weeks at a time, and then get upset when she would find her at Autumn's house. Maylee was punished whenever her Aunt Autumn was mentioned.

Once Maylee was about twelve years old, Candace finally gave up and no longer asked about her or showed any concern. Candace couldn't care less whether Maylee came home or not. Candace knew that Autumn's was the only phone number Maylee knew by heart, and that's where she would usually be. There was no point in the chase. Besides, the less Maylee was around, the more freedom there was for her. There were no whiny voices begging for food, or phone calls from teachers complaining about smelly clothes or random bruises.

Candace now stared back at her angry sister contemplating what insult she would throw next. Whether it be about Keith dying, or about their Mom being in a nursing home, she usually thought of the things that would hurt Autumn the most before she spoke.

"You're not going to find her, Autumn. All you're going to do out there is waste what little money you have left and abandon Mom. You're leaving her here to rot while you chase a ghost."

Candace watched closely and fully satisfied as Autumn winced. The fact that their mother would be left all alone pulled fluid to the surface of her eyes. Hannah Brown, Autumn and Candace's mother had lived with Autumn for quite some time after her stroke. Once she became too heavy for Autumn to lift, Hannah was checked into the nicest nursing home within a twenty-mile range. Autumn would visit her on a regular basis. Candace, on the other hand, hadn't seen their mother in years.

Autumn watched her sister strut to the door, then turn to look back as she twisted the door's handle. "Good luck on your mission, Superwoman." Candace sneered, chuckled lightly, and walked out.

Lightning Source UK Ltd.
Milton Keynes UK
UKHW012047040920
369381UK00004B/119